PAINTED CITIES

PAINTED CITIES

ALEXAI GALAVIZ-BUDZISZEWSKI

MCSWEENEY'S

SAN FRANCISCO

MᶜSWEENEY'S
SAN FRANCISCO

www.mcsweeneys.net

Cover illustration and lettering by Joel Trussell

Some of this work appeared in different form in *Third Coast, Alaska Quarterly Review, Triquarterly, Ploughshares, Chicago Noir, Indiana Review, River Styx, Fourteen Hills, X Connect,* and *New American Writing* 30.

McSweeney's and colophon are registered trademarks of McSweeney's, a privately held company with wildly fluctuating resources.

Printed in Michigan by Thomson-Shore.

ISBN: 978-1-938073-80-9

So put me on a highway
And show me a sign
And take it to the limit one more time
                                    —Eagles

DAYDREAMS

My memories come in negative. My mother had a box of photographs, but I don't recall ever seeing any of them. Instead, what I recall are her negatives: the orange-tinted strips of color film that she kept tucked in the developers' envelopes. Some of these envelopes she'd labeled—CHRISTMAS 1974; FLORIDA 1972. Others she hadn't, and she would lift these out of the photo box and say, "All right, let's see what these are from." She always went for the negatives, never the actual prints.

My memories compete with reality. I know my uncle Juan had a cream-colored Lincoln. We waxed it every fall, every spring. I used to sit in the backseat while my uncle cruised with his girlfriend, Letty. They hardly spoke a word, only listened to music: the O'Jays, Earth, Wind and Fire. Sometimes my uncle would look back at me. Then Letty would look back too, and then they would look at each other, and smile.

When it was dark and we had dropped Letty off, I used to sit in the front seat and stare at the glowing dashboard. The warm smell of summer always poured in through the open windows, even when we stopped at a red light or stop sign. In the flood of streetlights, my legs would turn a bright orange and I would wonder if I was going to get a sunburn. We'd drive a little longer. I'd try to guess where we were by the tops of the apartment buildings. I never knew when we had actually returned home. My uncle would say, "Okay, man, let's go." And only then would I know that we had parked and that the ride was over.

I remember all this vividly, our summer nights, but really, all I can recall is what it *felt* like. I try to piece together *image* from that. When I try to think of image, what I see is the light blue of my uncle's skin, the silver black of his Dago T-shirt. What comes to mind is a glaring white night sky, a glaring white dashboard, luminescent, bright opaque, an opaque so bright you want sunglasses, but then you realize anything dark is just as bright, and you're helpless. What comes to mind are my uncle's dark teeth as he smiles, frightening, outlined in white, like ghost images. And I can see through my uncle, his ice-blue skin. I can see the tuck-and-roll of the driver's side door. I can see the darkness of the chrome door handle and window lever, all this in complete reverse, like an x-ray image.

When I was seven or eight, there was cotillion in my family. My cousin Irene had just turned fifteen. My sister, Delia, who was only a year older than me, was selected to participate as a *dama*, and my cousin on my father's side, Little David, was selected as her escort, her *chambelán*.

The girls wore pink outfits. I don't remember this, but in the basement of our old house, my sister's pink gown hung in a plastic sheath throughout my childhood. My sister wore a corsage, and a pink headband to keep her hair back. These things I also don't remember, but there was a negative, a photograph of my sister and Little David, together in front of the house we used to live in.

In the negative, her gown is purple. In the negative, everything pink is a deep, luscious purple, a purple I've never seen before or since, bright, yet at the same time thick and heavy. David, in his tuxedo, is only his reverse: wide lapels, black coat with tails. Stuck in his left lapel is a fat carnation, dark, like a bundle of black roses. And his teeth are glowing. In the negative, David's teeth are glowing, the way my uncle's used to late at night, when we cruised our neighborhood.

There was a shootout at the cotillion. My cousin Irene was dating a Morgan-Boy and a rival street gang had shown up, friends of one of the guests. I didn't know where my father was. I didn't know where my sister was, or David. But my mother took me underneath the table and held my head in her lap and covered my ears. I remember the gunshots. I remember the screaming.

Eventually my mother let me lift my head. The white table-cloth draped around us like long curtains. My mother opened her purse, and beneath the table, with gunshots ringing off the walls of the church basement, my mother pulled out an envelope of photographs. "All right," she said. "Let's see what these are from." And against the glowing white of the tablecloth's edge, we held up our orange strips of celluloid and saw things that weren't there, colors that didn't exist.

1817 S. MAY

My sister and I used to pan for gold. We used to squat along the curb of May Street, with the frying pans our landlady, Betty, would let us use, and sift through the water that flowed from the fire hydrant that our upstairs neighbor, Joe, would open up whenever it was especially hot out. I can remember scooping up mounds of grit from the gutter and turning it over and over in small seesawing circles, convinced that I would one day strike it rich. I suppose, in all our days of panning, if Delia and I had turned in all the glass we collected, all the bottle tops and all the can tabs we found, we might have become millionaires, but probably not. Still, as we made up our separate mounds of would-be valuables, depositing our finds in coffee cans labeled GOLD, SILVER, and DIAMONDS, filling each one up with bottle tops, can tabs, and broken glass, respectively, we thought of how we could one day buy a mansion for my mother, a Jaguar for my father, and how we could leave our apartment to our uncle Pepe, who slept in our pantry along with the *chiles* and *frijoles*.

I don't know where, on the South Side of Chicago, Delia and I got the idea to start panning. It did not seem instinctual, like I later realized looking behind my back every few steps was—something inherently South Side. But we panned for gold nonetheless, devoutly, often consuming entire afternoons sifting through the cold water that flowed like swift-moving streams down the gutters of May Street. Eventually our panning became so routine that when Joe from upstairs would crack open the fire hydrant on those sweltering days when the humidity weighed upon our heads like torture, Betty would simply leave the pans we used outside her first-floor apartment. The moment Delia and I were allowed out, we would race down our apartment building's steps, scoop up our pans mid-stride, and burst out onto May Street, where we would take up our positions along the running water and begin to sift and pour.

Until our panning, the main attraction on such hot days was watching the older kids play in the huge domes of water they would create with the pumps. An utter mystery for me until well into my youth was what old tires were doing wrapped around all the fire hydrants. Then, early one summer, I caught the older kids of my block wedging a board between the tire and the mouth of our hydrant, creating a ramp, a deflector for the sheer rush of water. The result was an explosion, a cascading bloom of water that when done right could reach the other side of May Street. I realized suddenly the ingenuity of the kids in my neighborhood.

There were battles to see which block reigned supreme, which block could build the most gargantuan dome of water. While there was never any organized contest, no official measurement, no agreed-upon rating system, whenever someone would walk down to a store on Eighteenth Street past the neighboring blocks, he would always return with vivid, detailed accounts of how the "dudes" over on Allport or Throop "got one that's *fucking huge*," and here he would spread his arms in some random inflated measurement. These words seemed to spark something in the residents of my block. When they heard them, they would all inherit the wide, bright eyes of the storyteller, and it would seem suddenly as if there were some greater purpose now, something to band together for—defeat of a neighboring block. So Joe from upstairs would be called, and he would come charging out, barefoot, in his cutoffs, squinting at the exhaust of the cigarette dangling from his mouth, carrying the heavy iron pump key—the tool that allowed him to open the hydrant—and he would slowly, professionally, crank up our water pressure, inflate our dome of water even higher. The valves would creak, beneath the sidewalk the water lines would shudder, everyone would wonder when Joe was going to stop, and then finally he would, and a cheer would go up, and Joe would retreat back upstairs, where I'm sure a Sox game and a six-pack of tall boys were waiting on him.

I felt quite proud that Joe, the miracle worker, he who could feather a pump's water pressure just enough to give us the most beautiful fire-hydrant creations ever, lived in our building. For the most part, though, and this is a side of Joe that tends to be overlooked, he spent his waking hours drunk or high. He would have loud parties that ended up in fistfights at 3 a.m., people falling down our three-flat's stairs, creative insults being slung in the stairwell, bottles being thrown on the front sidewalk. Delia and I were often awoken by Joe's scuffles, and we would look out our front window to see Joe out there either pounding on or being pounded by some similar-looking heavyweight. My father would call the cops (if Betty downstairs hadn't already) and things would be settled. Joe would crawl back upstairs, we would crawl back into bed, and all would be forgotten. It was routine. Joe gets loud, someone calls the cops, Joe apologizes with a sincere, smiling face to my mother and Betty the next day.

At times, when summer was in full swing and the pump contests were unofficially under way, the block just down from us, just across Nineteenth Street, would try and outdo us with its own fans of water. It occurs to me now that we really had no name for these fans of water. All one had to say was "Man, look at *that* one," and it was obvious to all those listening that another oasis had been spotted, another reprieve in our neighborhood's desert of concrete. To stand beneath one of these great formations, within its massive dome of water, was to be in a completely different world, secluded, excluded, soundless except for the roar of the rushing water. Even the kids standing right next to you could not be heard, though you could see that their mouths were moving, that they were screaming just like you. The test was to see who could stand to be beneath the dome the longest. And then, upon exiting, the most excruciating task of all was to become real again. You would run to someone, the first person you saw, and start bragging about how great it was to have been beneath the dome so long. Or, if you were younger, as I was, you would run full speed to your mother, and act as if you had just performed some great feat of courage, some act beyond human comprehension, like the scaling of a monstrously high chain-link fence, the rescue of a baseball from a dog-infested yard, anything to get a reaction, a confirmation that you were there, that people could hear you and that you could hear them. At any one time during those summers, there were hordes of lost individuals, newly escaped from the great domes of water, running around frantic, trying to reestablish some sense of *being* in the real world.

From where our pump was, the kids down the block looked like miniature figurines, pet people running about, yapping, like windup toys. They were our block's biggest rivals, and they had their own Joe, a fat man who would walk out with a pump key and turn up their water pressure whenever dominance needed to be established. Often, their routine, their unspoken challenge, was to turn up the pressure of their pump and wait for a response from us. Then Joe would come out, determined, nonchalant with confidence, and the domes of water would begin to rise in battle. Their group would cheer when theirs got higher. We would cheer when Joe got ours higher. The valves would screech; within our cracked sidewalk the pipes would moan like the hull of a sinking ship. We would cringe at every turn of Joe's wrench. Inevitably, at least from what I remember, Joe would feather out just enough water pressure so that we never reached our breaking point—the point at which our board snapped in half and shot out across the street with enough speed to kill someone. But just in case, when our battles with the next block began, everyone left the area of water flow and fell in behind Joe, where we could cheer in safety.

We always won. The block down from us had a history of shoddy pump construction. The minute theirs would give, they would all yell in disappointment. Sometimes a little voice could be heard echoing down the block—"Next time, assholes, we'll get you next time."

And they would set to building their dome up once again—runners sent off in search of new boards, water pressure inched back up to a respectable level. Joe would accept congratulations, restore our pump's normal flow, and everything would resume, things would go back to normal: kids running in and out of the water, experiencing sudden losses upon entering and desperate struggles upon exiting.

There was a layer of grit settled at the bottom of May Street's gutters, and possibly, this is what sparked the idea to start panning. Maybe, at some point, one of us had scooped up a handful of this grit and suddenly discovered diamonds and precious minerals. Maybe one of us had looked at the other with the astonished face of a scientist who has just made an inadvertent discovery—a face of excitement—a face filled with the feelings one tries to quell by saying, "Wait a minute. I need to try this again." And maybe we did try again, and came up with more jewels and riches, and soon this prompted us to start panning, like early Californians—ghetto forty-niners.

At first we must've looked like fools, Delia and I, leaning over the curb, sifting through the heavy till of the gutters. But soon we became pioneers, and it was not long before the other kids of our block began prospecting as well: Little Joey from the apartment building next door and his sister, Genie; Mario León, the son of the corner grocer; and even Peety, the eight-year-old pool-shark, whose father owned the corner tavern. I seem to remember Delia saying to me once, "They're taking all our gold," but I am not sure if this is actual memory. Though this seems like something my sister would have said (she was the more enterprising of the two of us), it seems also that Delia and I almost never spoke while we did our panning; rather, we just squatted there, elbows between our knees, hands turning over and over, primed to pluck our riches.

Gold was, of course, the most sought-after of the precious commodities we panned for. But often we found diamonds and silver as well. Delia, when she would come across those rare green diamonds (shattered pieces of a 7UP bottle), or those blue ones (who knows what these were from), would hold them up to the sunlight and squint like a jeweler; then she would plunk them in the appropriately labeled coffee can and grunt, as if saying to herself, *Damn, now that was a good one.* I, on the other hand, often skipped over the diamonds, and instead focused in on the gold—those gold-colored 7UP bottle caps, preferably the ones with the red 7UP insignia still visible on them. But Delia, glitter queen that she was, went for the diamonds, the glass, and always had Band-Aids on her fingers because of it. This became a precautionary measure for her after a time, and I am sure that if my mother had ever found out what was happening to all the Band-Aids, she would have forbade us from ever prospecting again. As it was, though, my mother had no idea, and Delia would wrap her fingers and dig in, pulling up colored glass, holding it to the sunlight, and occasionally looking over at me with the sparkle in her eyes that I came to understand as my sister daydreaming about what she would do with our fortune.

We discussed our plans late at night in the bed we shared. Much to the disgust of Delia, my ideas on what we would do with our fortune focused more on family matters: how a move up to a mansion might benefit our other family members, for example, Pepe moving out of the pantry and taking over the apartment, and my cousin Chuey, who often slept on our kitchen floor when his wife kicked him out, moving in to the pantry. There were other ideas as well: how we might purchase a van for my uncle Max, so his *chile*-delivering business could prosper, how we could pay for my aunt Chachie to become a doctor and guarantee ourselves free medical care for the rest of our lives. These were all even trades, I figured, arrangements that would in some way benefit each one of us. But Delia had different ideas— ideas that seemed more along the lines of what millionaires might really do with their fortunes.

"A pool," she would say as we lay there in the dark. "For the back of the mansion, we have to have a pool. And a dug-in one too, like they have in *The Beverly Hillbillies*." And when Delia would say this I would imagine her eyes lighting up like they always did when she thought of such amazing things. At times, there in the dark, I turned to see if the walls on her side of the bed had actually lit up with the glow.

Our apartment on May Street was a reflection of the street itself— small and cramped. It was for this reason that Delia and I slept in the same bed, and shared a room with my parents, and why my uncle slept in our pantry. I suppose if we had all sat down and thought about it, someone would've come to the conclusion that "Gee, this apartment is too small," but the thought never entered our minds— or maybe it did. Maybe it was always there, lingering, when I would fall asleep on my uncle's mattress in his pantry/bedroom and he would kick me out because there wasn't enough room for the both of us, when we had to turn our mattresses up so that my parents' party guests wouldn't spill beer on them or singe them with cigarettes, when my cousin Chuey would come over, drunk, kicked out of his own apartment up the block, and fall asleep facedown on our kitchen floor. Delia and I would eat cold cereal and watch Saturday-morning cartoons as he slept at our feet, snoring, moaning, gyrating his pelvis as if having nasty dreams. There were no problems then. For us it was all routine.

And maybe our entire block felt the same. Maybe the entire neighborhood, with its towering church steeples, its neon signs, its liquor stores all crammed together like they were missing space to breathe, maybe everyone who lived there felt that way. So much so that the crampedness, the density, was just another thing you "understood," like the humidity during the summer, like the fact that Joe or any of the other drunks or dope addicts might need the cops called on them, like the feeling that we needed to get into pump battles with the people on the next block. The fact that I could hear Little Joey's parents, in the apartment building next door, arguing about how Joey's father slept with other women, never entered my mind. The fact that my parents screamed about what was happening to all our money, then turned around and made discreet love on the other side of our bedroom, wasn't a bother. I noticed, but mostly I didn't. Mostly at night, when all the families in the neighborhood would get to arguing and sex, I would lie with Delia and talk about fortunes, about pools and about great schemes that would affect each member of my family forever. All these things, these feelings of crampedness, these feelings of being locked down in close quarters, simply *were*. They were undeniable facts that fell so far back in the mind one could sit on the front stoop and drink a cold beer, or, in the case of the younger kids on the block, squat on the curb and pan for gold.

Back then, it seems, there was something more romantic about living in a ghetto, in poverty, with too many members of your family; or maybe I was simply too young to have made an honest distinction between what was real—the gunshots, the suspicious fires, the deaths—and what was fake, or imaginary—the precious jewels, the gold Delia and I used to strike in the gutters. I've tried explaining out loud to myself that any person, any child, with imagination enough, need enough, to turn chips of broken glass into diamonds, bottle tops into gold, certainly has enough imagination to reverse the entire situation of his youth, turn it all into a fairyland of lowriders, loud radios, sexy women with long dark hair, short-shorts, and deep red lips. But the fact remains that May Street was a place where I saw drunken men brawling to the death, I saw wives get beat by their husbands, I saw children get hit by cars and then watched those cars get chased down by neighbors and the drivers get beat into bloody pulps.

Early one summer morning Delia and I were awakened by my parents and told to get out of the building. I remember distinctly the smell of smoke, the sound of sirens and the distorted chatter of police radios. I remember also, distinctly, being convinced that someone had set our apartment building on fire, thinking to myself, *What did we do?* and running through a list of possible reasons why someone might have wanted to burn our place down—*Has my father been cheating on my mother? Did Joe mess up a drug deal?* As I ran down the stairs, led by my uncle, followed by Delia and my parents, I remember thinking also that something must be saved, that a dog or cat *must* be rescued. And though I am sure I got this idea from some TV commercial for fire alarms, or some newscast of a suburban rescue of a cat or dog, some middle-class situation far removed from the reality of May Street, I still felt there was something I needed to save.

When we got to the front of the building and turned to look in the direction of the flames, we saw that it wasn't our building that was on fire, but the building behind. And with faces of relief, and glassy eyes, each family from May Street's row of apartment buildings stood looking at the flames shooting up.

Betty our landlady was already out there, hard at work, sweeping the cascading soot into the gutter, the soot that kept falling over the places she had just swept. And Joe was out there as well, undoubtedly thinking up some way to snag one of the pump keys the firemen were using. I remember when word was passed that it had been Lil' China who had set the blaze. That he had done so in a jealous attempt to get back at his ex-wife for seeing another man. I remember also the gasps that sounded from everyone but Betty, who was too busy sweeping her sidewalk, when it was further discovered that Cookie, China's ex-wife, and their three kids had not been able to escape the fire. It was in this instance especially, this milling around of all the neighbors, the good-looking women revealed in their curlers and eyebrowless faces, the kids in their Loony Tunes pajamas, the fathers, like mine, in their shorts, shirtless, bare, that I remember hearing all the phrases that made up my youth, and surely Delia's too. "Who was it?" "Did they catch him?" "Did she die?" "Damn, the kids too?" All these phrases delivered with honest concern, with heartfelt sincerity. In the eyes of all those neighbors, looking up, you could see the flames, and you could also see that just like Delia and I thought about fortunes while we panned for gold, our neighbors were thinking about Cookie, her kids, and even China, who was now, it was reported, in custody. They could see flames rushing through their own apartments, engulfing their own families, and they could see perfectly how the cops had beat China once he was caught, "because any father who kills his kids would definitely get his ass beat by the cops." And somehow, though China's deed was inherently wrong, it was obvious that everyone there could fathom it completely. In light of China, the death of Cookie, in light of all those other deaths—Smokey who had been gunned down across the street one September night, or any of those others on the receiving ends of bullets or suspicious fires, or even those who had succumbed to natural deaths, to old age or heart attacks—in light of all this, the families could band together, the neighbors could all come together and say "Damn, the kids too?" and shake their heads with some common understanding, some relief in the thought that they had dodged yet another bullet, then say good night to each other in common courtesy, and retreat back to their apartments, like nothing could be done, like life was simply an arrangement, the cards had been dealt and you had to play.

Eventually, after the fire was quelled, and the firemen had given the all clear, my family climbed back up our stairs. By that time the sun was coming up, and my father asked us if we all wanted to go out onto the back porch, which faced east, toward a Lake Michigan masked by skyscrapers, toward a sunrise that would bring the usual heat wave, and toward the charred buildings that had been affected by the blaze. We stood out there, Delia, my parents, my uncle, and I, looking at the burnt remains, inhaling the deep smell of seared wood, basking in whatever coolness the early morning offered. We looked at the wet streets, the buildings dripping with black, sooty water, and I suppose we were searching for something. As the sun came up, and the morning mist began to burn off, I looked down the long rows of porches that stretched off into infinity on either side of us, and saw each family, arms entwined, looking toward the sunrise and doing the same.

PAINTED CITIES

HANGING GARDENS

Rom has his colors down like no one else in the hood. Turned the west face of Speedy's corner store into a three-dimensional dreamscape, complete with galaxies, shooting stars, and black holes that appear to bore right through the brick wall they're sprayed on. How he gets his colors to catch light like that, especially at night, when the orange of the streetlamps reflects off his murals in iridescent gleams, is a mystery to everyone. Awestruck, they watch him perform, red bandanna maroon with sweat, clothes and skin speckled with over-spray: baby blue, crimson red, hi-glo yellow.

Speedy had seen the job Rom did on the alley wall of Saint Stephen's rectory. The Christ on the cross mural: overpowering not because of the crown of thorns, the blood-dripping wounds, or the long, pouting stare Catholics are accustomed to, but because of the way Christ looms above, as if frescoed on the concave surface of a spoon. Around Christ galaxies spin, shooting stars streak, and his white gown flows in a cosmic wind. To this day the mural is a routine stop on the North Side's bus tours into the heart of the city.

Most of Rom's pieces are commissioned by area businesses or churches—maybe even the public, if Rom takes to heart the suggestions he hears while working. "Hey, bro, how about dedicating to my girlfriend, Flaca?" "How about to my mother?" "My grandmother who died yesterday?" But his dedication to Arelia Rosas, a ten-year-old girl who disappeared the summer before last, simply appeared one morning without warning on the octagonal brick kiosk that sits before the old Lutheran church on Nineteenth and Peoria.

The neighbors called the mural "poignant," though many were unsure of what the word meant. It wasn't negative, though, most were sure of that, so they used the word over and over to describe the dedication until months later, when the word dropped from favor through sheer overuse.

In the mural, a caricature of Arelia sits alone on the wood bench her grandfather made for her many years before and placed in front of the ground-floor apartment he lived in. How Rom knew this intimate detail of the Rosas family, no one knows, but they chalk it up to an artist's intuition. Anyone passing the scene sees the bench, the brick-molded asphalt siding of her grandfather's building, and knows immediately the moment takes place in summer, that there is an open fire hydrant somewhere nearby and that the scents of the neighborhood—frying tacos, boiling pots of garlic-spiced *frijoles*, cool Lake Michigan breezes transported by miles of sewer pipe—layer the atmosphere.

She sits playing with her hair. Everyone remarks how Arelia could just sit for hours, contented, smiling to herself occasionally when something funny came to mind. "But she never cried," her mother says. "No, never." Yet in the dedication, as contented as Arelia seems, chrome tears run down her high cheeks. This is where poignancy takes place.

Within the basket of each tear a city appears, like a hanging garden. Upon close inspection the image is revealed as a portrait of the neighborhood itself, shot from above, minute down to steeples and the path of the L as it snakes down Twenty-First Street. How he got his spray down to such fine points no one will ever know, and this is an issue of contention among the local graffiti artists: whether or not Rom actually broke the rules and employed brush. But the haze is there, the over-spray, the telltale sign of aerosol art, which, in this case, enhances the already translucent tears, the cities held within glass bulbs like holiday paperweights filled with liquid, begging to be flipped and allowed to snow.

The tears don't stop at the cheeks. They continue to fall: two are in midair. Eventually, one glances off Arelia's white knee and multiplies in a flash, producing more tears, finer tears, smaller cities. The silver droplets reach the image's painted cement sidewalk and sink into what now appears to be a vast city in and of itself, splayed out beneath the reflective sheen of Arelia's black patent-leather shoes. Corridors of streetlights, side streets, meet at infinite points around the kiosk. At times, the neighbors say, the painted cities come alive, movement can be seen, the L's slithering like hobby railroads. The neighborhood's lowriders stop and go on the boulevards.

Rom takes no credit for his murals. Never signs them, unless somewhere in the jumble of letters at the bottom of his pieces the name ROM is encoded. The neighbors call this humility, though many are unsure of what the word means. They use it anyway, while they wait for miracles.

RESIDUE

C ould've been Death himself, the grim reaper, descending into the basketball court that night. Could've been ready to pull out any number of weapons, automatics, pumps, side-by-sides—everyone knows the grim reaper don't use sickles no more.

Grim reaper *looked* like he grew up South Side, way he pimped down the alley ramp into Barrett Park. Even though ol' boy was walking slow, that slight bump in his step was all South Side, Twenty-Second and Damen to be exact. Could name the street corner by that walk alone.

First thought was he'd been living in somebody's basement. Jose Morales, valedictorian at Juarez High School, thought it, and Sleepy too, twelve-year-old, droopy eyed Party Boy in training. Everyone in the park that night thought it. That, and how the world got awful small sometimes. Like just last week, when Beany from the Two-Ones found out his old lady was fucking some dude where she worked downtown. Xerox repairman wound up being Juice from the Party People over on Allport, Beany's best friend when they came up together on Eighteenth. Two days later Juice was found tied to an alley lamppost, alive but beaten. Beany's out hunting for his old lady now; he's got something more serious in mind for her.

Jr. Chine stood at the far end of the basketball court watching the scene develop. He wasn't afraid of anything he could see, at least that's what he liked to tell himself. He'd heard Juice's story, how Beany was now after his girlfriend. "Motherfuckers should've seen it coming," he'd told Joker, his Party Boy brother, his best friend in the neighborhood. "You look for trouble, shit's going to find you first." Joker's only response had been to laugh. Joker was a thief, of everything.

But it figured the grim reaper was living in the neighborhood. Probably renting out a musty concrete basement for a buck fifty a month, utilities included, stolen from a next-door neighbor. Might have assumed the name Julio Ramirez, or Juan Calderon, one of those generic Mexican names nobody'd suspect it was Death himself, coming in at strange hours. Whoever owned the building, the landlord living in the front, highest apartment, like they always do, probably thought Death was just a good worker. Probably thought he was some *mojado* busting his ass making calculators in Elgin for fourteen hours a day, wiring cash back home to Mexico, supporting seven growing children and a wife named Iris, or Esmeralda, some name that brought to mind young beauty, though she herself was tired and worn. Landlord probably thought to hire Death too, being he was such a good worker. Give him twenty bucks to patch the front sidewalk, holes so big kids be falling down there, assumed kidnapped until someone heard the screaming.

And all along it was the grim reaper, filling in holes, living in the neighborhood, existing incognito.

Jr. Chine said it first, to no one in particular: "Hey, bro, that's Joker." Exactly how he knew the grim reaper was really Joker was impossible to tell, but they were good friends, and good friends can generally sense one another, like when you know a hit's pulling down the street five minutes before you actually see the car, cab darker than the street itself, orange street light thick as humidity.

It had been Jr. Chine's shot. He'd had the ball on the low post, about to release his patented baseline jumper, dramatic for its disregard of the backboard, its confidence as it cycled through the air and then swooped the chain-mesh net. The ball dropped from his hands like a whistle'd been blown. It trotted toward the field house, down the slope of the compressed basketball court, each bounce accompanied by the twang of an overinflated ball, into the slot between the cyclone retaining fence and the back of the brick building, where ball players, drunks, and wicky-stick fiends pissed, the piss collecting over generations, reeking, giving the field house its neighborhood moniker, "Stinky."

The figure's hands were hidden in his sweatshirt pockets. The deep hood hung low over his brow and his arms were locked at the elbows. The material was being stretched down as if the figure were cupping his balls, making the body seem even more ominous, an open mouth screaming, melting. If the crowd on the court could've seen the hands, a positive identification could've been made. They would've known for sure it was Death: long, white fingers, black fingernails. Or they would've known it was really Joker: bleeding crucifix tattoo on the web of his right hand, PARTY BOYS etched in Old English script like a banner over the crucifix. Jr. Chine approached the descending figure cautiously, his own right hand gripping the .25 automatic stuffed in the pocket of his cutoff jeans. He flipped the safety off, though, like always, he questioned immediately whether he'd actually flipped it on, and was now about to die feeling stupid. If he lived, he vowed, he'd memorize which action was the correct one, get the safety situation down pat, like he had the clip-loading maneuvers down pat, practicing for hours as he lay in bed, popping the clip in and out, in the dark, sightless, the clicks of the release mechanism like second nature. He sidestepped toward the figure. His steps shortened as he neared. And suddenly Jr. Chine's vision went third-person. Everything—the game, those standing behind, the cigarette Jr. Chine had left smoldering until he was back downcourt—disappeared from view, and he could see it all as if he was living his own movie.

"Joker, what the fuck are you doing?" Jr. Chine said. And a tiny voice came from the hooded figure.

"Hey, bro, we need to find Angel."

"Who the fuck are you?" Jr. Chine said, now loud and boisterous, his adrenaline sky-high. He bobbed and weaved as he moved around the figure. "Take off that hood so I can hear you." Jr. Chine's hands were wet. His right hand around the grip of the gun had become cold, though the rubber grip itself remained hot. He pulled the gun from his pocket and held it stiff-armed at his leg.

"It's me, bro," the voice said a little louder, the hooded head following Jr. Chine as he juked and stuck.

"Joker?" Jr. Chine asked.

"Yeah."

Jr. Chine cocked his body, ready to spring into action, then reached out and peeked under the hood. It *was* Joker, though with all the welts, the fluvial bruises around his eyes, the fresh slices to his cheeks, it was hard to tell. Jr. Chine's trigger arm went limp, his elbow finally unlocked after what had felt like hours. Vision reeled itself back in. The burning in his arm remained, but he relaxed and put the small gun back in his pocket.

"Hey, bro," Joker said. "Angel's on his way to kill Susan."

"Susan who?" Jr. Chine said.

"His lady, bro."

UNDERGROUND

There are cities down there, Little Egypt said so. He said they're smaller cities, not nearly as many people, but they have traffic and L's, just like we do up here.

The subway used to connect. Little Egypt said that too. That the Douglas-Park B Line used to take a steep dive right after LaSalle Street and descend into the cities below, neighborhoods stacked on top of one another deep into the earth, like department-store floors. "But then," he said, "they built downtown, John Hancock and all that. Now the subway just flies right over, Jackson Boulevard, Monroe. People up here don't even care anymore."

I saw Little Egypt's suitcase once. He kept it stored beneath his bed, packed and ready to go if he ever got the call to leave. "My grandfather took this baby all around the world," Little Egypt said; he hoisted the suitcase onto his bed. "Should handle a trip below, I'd think." He patted the swollen hide, then curled out his bottom lip and nodded.

Inside were a lot of shorts. On the underside of the top flap a ziplock bag had been taped. A thick purple cross had been drawn on it, and beneath the cross, FIRST AID was written in large block letters. He untaped the bag and split the seal. Band-Aids, gauze, a spray-can of Bactine, a pamphlet on snake bites poured out over his blue comforter. A few sets of chopsticks from Jade of the East Chinese spilled out as well. I lifted a set. Along the paper wrapper JADE OF THE EAST was written in familiar Oriental script. A local address followed, then a picture of a Chinese temple, layered, like a playing-card house.

"That's my grandmother's favorite restaurant," Little Egypt said. He took the set of chopsticks from me and tore off the temple end. He split the sticks. "They make great splints." He placed one along his thin forearm. "And communication tools." He tapped out Morse code: "SOS," he whispered. "And great weapons too." He did a pirouette, then waved the chopsticks in my face. "Hi-ya," he snarled. "But they don't really fight down there." He straightened and put the chopsticks back in their paper sleeve. "Really, it's a more peaceful society."

Double-D batteries were taped like shotgun shells along the inside wall of the suitcase. From between his piles of T-shirts and shorts he pulled a red plastic flashlight. He offered it to me and I flicked it on, casting a sharp yellow beam against his white wall. "I've had that puppy for years," Egypt said. "Never failed me. Not once." He curled out his lower lip again and shook his head. "Never." I flicked off the lamp and handed it back to him, grip first, the way one does a pistol or switchblade. "I mean, they have lights down there and everything," Little Egypt said. He tucked his flashlight back in between his clothes. "But it's better to be safe than sorry." He pulled a roll of clear packing tape from a bureau drawer and retaped the first-aid kit to its position on the underside of the top flap.

Sometime later, one morning before school, Little Egypt was at my door, suitcase at his side. He was dressed in his church clothes: a red knit sweater, tan slacks, brown loafers so polished they seemed wet. It was early spring, the sun was unusually high and bright.

"Just wanted to say bye," Egypt said. He smiled, his row of tiny teeth nearly fluorescent. I offered to walk him, and I quickly dressed and washed my face. Over the running water of our kitchen sink, I heard Egypt on our front stoop, whistling.

We walked down May Street.

"I left a note for my grandmother," Little Egypt said. "She should see it when she gets back from church. I'll write her, of course. I just didn't want to be too specific, tell her exactly where I'm going. Sometimes," Little Egypt said, "a man just has to break free." I nodded.

We passed the graffiti-covered field house of Dvorak Park, the pool, shards of broken glass catching sunlight along the concrete deck.

"That's one thing I won't miss," Little Egypt said, looking to the pool. "The pollution. They got a system down there, you know. Cleans all the streets. They never even *heard* of graffiti." He gave a nod as if there were a valuable lesson in this. Our field house's shower-room walls held messages: *Ambrose Love. Flaca, You Know I Still Love You, Junebug.*

At Twenty-First Street we turned the corner and walked toward the abandoned junkyard. "Well," Egypt sighed. He put his suitcase down. "I guess this is it." He stuck out his hand. "I'll be sure to write, and I hope to see you again sometime." He clicked his tongue twice and winked. Then he lifted his suitcase, turned, and walked down the quiet street. As he walked, the heavy suitcase bounded off his short leg; he held out his opposite arm like a cantilever. I realized then how small he was.

He stopped halfway down the block in front of the junkyard office. He stepped off the curb to a familiar sewer grate, one I myself had looked into often as I combed our neighborhood for loose change. The smell of wet metal spilled over the junkyard's corrugated walls—rust, oil. In the distance an L rumbled across Eighteenth Street, traffic whined on the Dan Ryan, a truck ground through its gears on Twenty-Second. I heard everything in echo, my ear to the city, one giant seashell.

"Hello!" Egypt called down into the grate. He was in a squat, his suitcase alongside him. He looked to me and smiled, then waved. The brown of his church shoes stood out red in the morning sun.

"Hello," he called again. "Anyone down there?" At that moment I realized I was about to lose my only friend.

THE CITY THAT WORKS

Puppet plays guitar. He strums his strings on Eighteenth Street and Wolcott, in the narrow gangway between Zefran Funeral Home and the El Milagro tortilla factory. There at night, the notes bounce up the brick walls around him and create an echo that Puppet believes he'll one day record and sell for millions of dollars.

He plays old tunes: Ritchie Valens ballads, Santo & Johnny's "Sleep Walk." He thinks he's romantic. When the L's rumble by, he continues playing, convinced somehow that his music is affecting the travelers: making a pickpocket reconsider as he slips his trigger hand toward a sleeping passenger's pocket.

Puppet can play the first few bars of Ritchie Valens's "Donna" like an expert. The rest he fumbles through, and he returns to the chorus like it's his lifeboat. The hair on the back of his neck stands on end. He wonders if those on the outside, those at either end of the dark gangway, where the orange of the streetlights glows in long, vertical slits, are feeling it too. Often, when he steps out of the gangway, he expects entranced crowds to be gathered there: beautiful women with tears in their eyes and a love for him undying. Of course, there never are—just the hum of the city at night, things on autopilot, neon signs, streetlights, the clicking of stoplights. Overhead another L rumbles by like a strip of film, only one or two of the yellow frames actually holding a silhouette.

Across the alley, in a bedroom on the top floor of a three-flat, a young girl sighs. She turns from her open window and faces the darkness. She hugs her pillow. "I love you, Ritchie Valens," she says. "I love you."

FREEDOM

I knew Buff before he was a Latin Count, before he was shot dead. His real name was David. I heard his aunt call him that once, when we were on top of the old pierogi factory. "David!" she called out. And Buff looked at me. "Shit," he said. He dropped the rock he had in his hand and went running across the gravel roof. He climbed over the air-conditioning unit and disappeared. I was up there alone then. I looked over the ledge onto Twenty-Second Street, the traffic. I looked at the kids playing swifties in the school playground across the street. I dropped my rock and climbed down as well. Throwing rocks wasn't fun unless you did it with someone.

David, or Buff, thought different. I had first met him a few months before, when my father had sent me to the A&P to get some milk. I was approaching the pierogi factory, just across Oakley Avenue. It was hot out that day; the sun felt somehow closer. *WHACK!* I heard. Across the street, a CTA bus screeched to a stop. The driver turned and stared back at me. Behind him, one of the large safety-glass windows had been shattered—a cool, spiderweb-like pattern spread over the entire pane. I looked to the sidewalk and continued walking. Finally, the bus moved on.

After it had crossed Western Avenue I turned and looked behind me. There, on the pierogi factory roof, standing at the ledge, was a boy my age, maybe a little younger, wearing a white T-shirt. His head was shaved. He had big ears and a smile that made him look something like Dopey from *Snow White*. He nodded at me as if he knew who I was.

"How'd you get up there?" I asked him.

"Around the back," he said. His speech was quick, almost hyper. At the end of his sentence he sucked his tongue, like he was fighting back saliva. Then he disappeared beyond the ledge.

I continued on to the A&P. I kept looking back. I imagined couches up there, tables, a secret hideaway. I was jealous. The pierogi factory roof was one of the last frontiers of my neighborhood. It was only two cinder-block stories high, but its remoteness, its sheer walls, made hiding up there seem equal to never having been born.

The second time we met we became friends. I had figured out how to get up onto the roof myself. The key was the chain-link fence that enclosed the factory's dumpster—at one corner the fence could be scaled, and then it was a matter of balance, a tightroper's balance, skirting lines of barbed wire to the factory's air ducts. After a leap to the thin sheet metal of the ducts, it was like climbing playground slides in reverse. Once, twice, three times, and suddenly you were there. It was amazing how easy it was. The pierogi factory roof had always seemed so impenetrable. I'd scaled garages. I'd scaled abandoned warehouse fire escapes. I'd even scaled the Western Avenue L stop, using the steel straps that held the support beams together as footholds. But I'd only ever dreamed about gaining the roof of the pierogi factory. That first time up there I surveyed the terrain: blank, empty, a white-gravel roof with a huge, green-painted air-conditioning unit. I was disappointed. Still, no one else I knew had ever been up there. Except, of course, for Buff, whose name I didn't even know yet.

It was a beautiful view, Twenty-Second Street, the street I lived on. I'd walked Twenty-Second so many times I knew every crack and buckle of its dilapidated sidewalks. But seeing it from two stories up, seeing each expanse of concrete imperfection, was awesome. The sidewalks seemed to make sense from up there; one could almost read the streets, the way they dipped and turned, how the sidewalk simply followed suit. I took a seat on the ledge of the roof and picked up a rock. I dropped it down to the sidewalk, waited for the sharp snap.

Across the street a large group of gangbangers, Disciples, were playing basketball. Their voices echoed loud and clear off the school building behind. "Ball! Ball!" they called out. "Foul, motherfucker! Goddamn!" It occurred to me that from up there I could be a spy if I wanted to. I could climb the roof late at night when the Disciples were having their meetings and overhear plans for drive-bys, cocaine sales, turf wars. It occurred to me that I could go to the Laflin Lovers or the Bishops, archrivals of the Disciples, and sell their secrets. I was hatching plans, schemes, when suddenly, behind me, the gravel churned.

He was there, standing. He was short, much shorter than he

looked from two stories down. He was younger-looking as well.

"Ha!" he said. "I knew it, bro! I knew you'd find the way up here." He sucked spit. "You climbed the fence, didn't you?"

"Yes," I said.

"Ha, I knew it!" he said. "No one else knows how to get up here. Just you and me."

I thought about this. In the end the climb hadn't seemed that difficult.

"Yeah," he said. "No one knows…"

He sat down next to me. He scooped up a handful of rocks. He had blue eyes. This was strange. He was Mexican, just like me; he had dark skin, dirty *summer* skin, but he also had these almost pastel-blue eyes. His face was lit up. He was smiling.

He shook his handful of rocks, loosing a couple. He looked down to the street. The noise of the basketball players came to us. "Center. Ball!" His eyes moved to the kids on the court.

"That's my cousin over there," he said. "Right there, see, the one with the ball." He looked down to his handful of rocks, shook another couple free. "His name is Junebug. He's a D. He's a little crazy."

I studied the kid with the ball. I'd seen him before. He looked like the type that liked to corner younger kids against the walls and ask them, "*What you be about?*" I avoided kids like him, crossed the street when I saw them coming.

"He shot me with a BB gun," Buff said. "Like three days ago." He pulled up his T-shirt and showed me. On his belly were three small welts, each holding a tiny, deep, dark pit in its center.

"He shot you?" I said.

"Yeah," Buff said. He laughed. He let his shirt down. "Ha ha, it didn't even hurt!" He looked down to his handful of rocks, shook out another two.

"You should go to the doctor," I told him.

"I should, right?" he said. "Aaaa."

Buff looked out over the ledge. By this time there was only one rock left from his handful. He looked far down the street.

"All right, bro, here it comes," he said. And then, in a split second, Buff jumped to his feet, fired his rock over the ledge, and ducked back down. I followed him, ducking too. I heard a loud *POP*, then a long screech of tires.

"Damn, bro, that was a cop car!" Buff said. "I got them, bro! I got the Law!"

I stayed low. I didn't want to see.

After a few moments I couldn't help it. If it *was* the cops, I thought it might be better if I turned myself in. I peeked over. Down on the street, a fat man wearing a red baseball cap was inspecting the shattered windshield of a rusted green station wagon. The man was dirty, sweaty, like he'd been working all day. His car didn't appear to have any backseats, only chunks of concrete filling the space from the driver's seat all the way to the tailgate. Stuck out of the back window was a bent metal pole with a red bandanna tied to its end. Two other people were down there, a couple. "*Pinche cabrones*," the man said. He shook his head and took his cap off. "*Pendejos*," he said. He rested his forearms on the roof of his car and then brought his head down. The couple walked away.

I tucked back down behind the ledge.

"It *was* the cops, *wasn't* it, bro?" Buff asked.

"Yes," I told him. "I think it was the narcs or something."

I swallowed hard.

"I knew it, bro," Buff said. "I knew it was the cops. My name is Buff," he said. He sucked spit.

"Jesse," I told him. I shook his hand.

That summer we were inseparable. I found out Buff was ten, the same age as me, although he looked like he could be a year younger, maybe even two. I found out that he lived on the North Side, but that he was spending the summer with his aunt on Twenty-Fourth Place because "people" were after him. I asked who the "people" were but he didn't want to tell me. He said: "Maybe you know them. I don't want to start any shit."

I also found out that Buff was going to be a father. That he had a girlfriend named Letty who occasionally visited him. She was seven months' pregnant, Buff said.

"Isn't your family mad?" I asked him.

"Yeah, but what are they going to do?" Buff said. "Besides, we're in love." I nodded like I knew love could be the reason for anything.

One afternoon we were up on the roof drinking some Cokes I had bought from Midwest corner store. I was staring up into the sky, listening to the traffic. Buff was looking over the ledge. We were talking about cars, maybe, or what prison was like. And then Buff said: "Look, there she is. There she is, bro. That's Letty." I turned and looked over the ledge. Across the street a group of girls were talking to some of the basketball players. "The one with the white shirt," Buff said. I looked to her. She was pretty. In fact, to me, at my age then, she was beautiful. She was thin, tall. She had short, dark hair. She looked like an older girl, like she was in high school. She smiled a lot, seemed genuinely happy about things. When she talked she moved her hands. When the boys spoke to her, she rolled her eyes. She did not look pregnant.

"That's Letty?" I asked Buff.

"Yeah, bro," he said. "I forgot to tell you she was coming down here today."

"She's talking to all those D's," I told him.

"I know," he said. "That's her cousins. Most of those guys down there."

I watched the girl move. I watched her pull back her hair as if she could put it in a ponytail. I heard her laugh out loud once. It was a deep laugh, like she had never been unhappy.

Finally, she and her friends walked away. When they were in the middle of the block Buff yelled out, "*Let-ty!*" He tucked down behind the ledge. "I don't want her to see me, bro," he whispered. "She doesn't like it when I call out her name like that." I lowered my head but continued to watch. The girl turned and looked behind her. In the playground the boys were already back to their game. She looked in front of her, across the street. She looked to her friends. They all laughed together.

"Did she look?" Buff asked.

"Yes," I told him.

"Damn, she knew it was me," he said. "She's going to be pissed later." He shook his head.

I rested my chin on the ledge and watched as the group of girls walked away. Buff came up and watched as well.

"Those girls are bitches," he said. "They talk too much."

This is how we spent our time. Sometimes throwing rocks, but mostly just talking. Buff showing me things, telling me what it was like to sniff cocaine. In truth, I don't think I believed much of what Buff said. I simply went along with it.

One afternoon he asked me if I'd ever smoked angel dust. "Yes," I said. "It's crazy, right?" Buff asked. "Yes," I answered.

I often wonder if Buff knew I was lying. But up on the roof, between the two of us, it didn't seem to matter. Sometimes I even question whether I actually spent a summer on that gravel roof, but then I think about what happened, and I know that I did.

The idea came to us at night. Back then my rule for coming home was the streetlights. When the streetlights came on I was to start heading home, no matter where I was. I followed the same rule when I was up on the roof, but I dawdled. I was only a block away from home. When I arrived and my father asked where I had been, I told him that I had been at Harrison Park, or some other place that took equally long to return from.

It was during the time the streetlights came on that we devised our plan. This was always quiet time. The time when the traffic changed from hectic shoppers and those returning home from work, to those simply cruising or heading out to parties. From the pierogi factory roof we could see clear over to California Avenue, where the mirror-windowed court building was lit up with the orange of the setting sun, the same color orange as the streetlights, which within minutes would flood up at us, shining over the ledge.

We lay there silently, on our backs, absorbing the heat of the day as it rose off the roof.

"Hey, bro," Buff suddenly said. "Wouldn't it be cool to live up here?"

I took a deep breath. I had my eyes closed. I felt as if time were holding still. "Yes," I answered.

"I was thinking maybe we could build a house up here," Buff said. "Like no one else would know. It would just be our secret."

I heard Buff move against the gravel, switching positions. I opened my eyes, looked up into the deepening purple sky.

"Maybe you and Letty could live up here," I told him. "Maybe we could even put a crib up here for your baby." I looked to Buff. He was leaning on one arm, looking down at me.

"Damn, that would be straight, right?" Buff said. "It would be like an apartment. We'd share it with you too. Like if you got a lady or something. I'd just tell Letty we had to go. You could have a dinner up here."

"Like candles and everything, right?" I asked him.

"Yeah, bro, just like that."

"But we'd need a table and chairs…"

"I know," Buff said. "And a bed, maybe a small table for the living room, some carpet or linoleum."

"Walls," I said. "And what about a roof…?" I considered the impossibility of the idea. Buff turned and looked out over the ledge. The streetlights were full power now; his face was bright orange. I closed my eyes. I thought about the hobos who lived under the bridge on Western Avenue. I thought about their homes, built of old doors, scraps of wood, sheets of metal. I opened my eyes again, looked into the nearly starless sky, the type of lonely sky one sees only in the city.

"Maybe we could find some wood," I said. I turned onto my side. "I know my father has a piece of metal, like a big tray. Maybe we could use that as a roof."

"That would be perfect, bro," Buff said. "I saw some wood the other day by the A&P."

"I could bring nails and a hammer," I said.

"I got some rope," Buff said.

"Cool," I replied, even though I wasn't sure what we'd need the rope for.

"Tomorrow," Buff said. "We'll start tomorrow."

I agreed.

That night I went home thinking of possibilities. When I walked through my door it was easily an hour and half after the streetlights had come on.

"Where the hell were you?" my father asked. His glare was familiar.

"At the park, playing basketball," I told him.

I felt a shift in his breathing. He was trying to keep himself from exploding.

"Did you win at least?" he asked.

"Yes," I said, and I quickly went to my room. I felt as if that was one of the last lies I'd ever tell my father.

The next day Buff and I met in the alley behind the factory. It was so early the neighborhood was still asleep, so early that what little traffic there was had time to echo between apartment buildings. Buff was holding a coiled-up line of dirty yellow rope.

"You want to get the wood first?" he asked.

"We should get that tray," I told him. "I don't know when my father will wake up."

"All right," Buff said. He put the rope around his neck like a sling, like a mountaineer ready for a climb. We walked the block back to my house. I let Buff in through the back gate, down into my gangway. The screen door that had fallen off last winter was up against the building next door. The front gate that had rusted free two summers ago was leaning against our building's back wall. Used tires that my father had plans to sell were stacked around the sewer cover. I unlocked the back door, then gave it a jolt with my shoulder—the only way the door would open. I led Buff down the stone steps into the basement. Led him past the furnace, past my bedroom, around the corner to where the tin sheet was.

"That's it, bro?" Buff asked.

"Yes," I said.

"That's perfect," he said.

He grabbed one side. I grabbed the other. We carried the piece of metal through the basement, our feet occasionally knocking against a corner, making a deep gong sound that I felt sure would wake my father upstairs.

When we got to the gangway I turned to shut my door.

"You got a nice house," Buff said. "Two floors and everything."

"It's not that nice," I said. "You should see the upstairs."

We walked the piece of metal back to the pierogi factory, leaned it against the cinder-block wall of the gangway. "I'll let the rope down," Buff said. And in a few minutes, above me, I heard Buff's voice.

"Ready?" he called down. He sucked spit like he always did. He tossed the yellow rope over the ledge. I took the end and wrapped the sheet metal as best I could.

"Okay," I told him.

And slowly, very slowly, the sheet of metal began to rise. I ran around the back, climbed the roof, and helped Buff pull it the rest of the way. We got the sheet to the top. We reached out and yanked the piece over the ledge. We sat on the gravel roof and breathed. A breeze was blowing now. Real traffic had started up on Twenty-Second Street. I looked at the rusted piece of metal and then looked to Buff. He was smiling, smiling the way he had that first time I met him. I smiled back. We were building a house now. It was only a matter of time.

The rest came easy. The wood Buff had found was really stacks of discarded truck pallets. We pulled them apart, pried off the healthy planks, scraped off the pieces of wilted lettuce and rotting tomato. We carried the planks three or four at a time back to the pierogi factory. After we tired of carrying, we hoisted them up to the roof and began construction.

After a few days the work became habit. In a week or so we had a solid frame. In another week the metal roof was in place, built of the tin sheet we had found in my basement and a piece of corrugated metal we'd discovered in a warehouse dumpster on Rockwell Avenue. Next we built the walls.

The room was small, maybe five by five. It was short, but tall enough for either of us to stand up in. Over the weeks of construction, the idea of having a separate living room and dining room had given way to what we were actually capable of: one single room. But really, that one room was enough. It was all ours.

The crowning achievement had been the mattress. Buff had

located it one morning while walking to the factory—to "work,"
as we had started to call it. He didn't even bother climbing the roof.
Instead, from the alley, he called up to me.

"I found a bed," he said. "Hurry before someone takes it."

Quickly, I slid down the air ducts. I walked the fence and then
jumped down to the alley. Together we ran the few blocks to where
Buff had spotted the mattress.

It was small. The mattress was from a cot or a child's bed. It was
sitting folded over in a dirt patch off the cement of the alley. I pulled
it open. It was stained in the middle, soiled like the mattresses in the
attic of my house, old mattresses left over from whoever had lived
there before, kids not potty-trained, old people unable to get up,
drunks. Buff must've seen the look on my face.

"This side it's not that bad," he said. He twisted the mattress so
I could see the back side.

He was right. The other side *was* cleaner.

We carried the mattress through the alleys of the neighborhood.
Every half block or so we set it down to adjust our grip. Other kids
from the neighborhood stopped their baseball games, their football
games, to let us pass.

Finally, we were home. We dropped the mattress in the gangway
of the pierogi factory. We rolled it up like a thick sausage. The
mattress smelled dank, sweet almost, like weeds in the sun, like an
alley in the summer.

Buff climbed the roof and let the rope down. I wrapped it around
the mattress. "Okay!" I called up to Buff. The yellow line went taut.

The bed was actually easier to lift than the piece of tin or even
the wood had been. The bed seemed to bounce right up the wall,

43

and when it got to the ledge, another strong jerk popped it right over onto the gravel roof. Immediately, we carried it into the house. We undid the knot and let it flop onto the floor. It was a perfect fit. The mattress lay snug against the rear wall, snug between the two side walls. Along the wall that held the doorway, there was enough space to walk in, enough space to put a table in if we wanted. Buff paced the small gap. He flapped his arms in and out as if doing the chicken dance.

"See, bro," he said. "In case we have parties."

I sat down on the bed. I sank down to the gravel. I forgot about the pee stains on the other side. The whole room took on the sweet smell of the dirty mattress. I leaned back and rested my head against the wall, our wall. Along the opposite side, sunlight piped in through cracks and nail holes in the planks. The wall looked like what I thought a nighttime sky in the country might look like, busy, crowded. I searched for constellations, the Big Dipper, the Little Dipper, ones I'd heard about in school. I closed my eyes.

"This is awesome, bro," Buff said.

"Yes," I said. "Awesome."

The fantasy lasted three days. Each night I was the one who called "time" and said we had to go. Each night got longer. I'm afraid of what might have happened had Buff never thrown that rock, the one that brought everything down. We were so close already, another day and maybe we would've stayed forever. Maybe we would've disappeared, like I wanted to back then, when I was young. Of course, things never work out the way you want them to. And then all you do, the rest of your life, is dream about what would've happened, or could've happened, had you done what you wanted to do in the first place.

In his defense, that rock was probably the biggest the gravel roof had to offer. In his defense, we should've hurled that rock months earlier, when the summer had first started, when I first met Buff. In his defense, no rock had ever glanced off a windshield, not like that, and really, what an odd set of circumstances, to have that little girl rounding third base in the park across the street at just the right time for the rock to go sailing into her temple, breaking her little head open, sending her chest-first into the concrete, her feet kicking up behind her, one lone white shoe cartwheeling over her body, landing somewhere up near her head, which had already begun to spout blood.

I remember this all as individual events. In my mind I can freeze each frame. Like when Buff and I turned to look at each other. Like when I saw Buff, not smiling but somehow shrugging, like he'd known this was going to happen, like he'd known something was going to happen to spoil everything.

They hadn't even seen us yet, the family of the little girl, the gangbangers across the street. They hadn't even called out like I remember them doing, *"Hey, up there! Look, there they are! There's those little fuckers!"* None of this had even happened yet when Buff turned to me and said, "Sorry." I wonder what he saw in my face. I wonder if he knew it wasn't just *his* fault, that we were accomplices, friends.

In another moment the gangbangers were on the roof. I was punched in the stomach hard enough to make my back ache.

"*Who threw the rock?*" one of them asked me.

I looked to Buff. "Me," he said. I am aware now that the noble thing would've been for me to say that I had done it, that *I* had thrown the rock. And I can see the nobility in Buff speaking up— even though he *had* done it, he didn't have to *say* he had done it. At the time, though, the thought of taking the blame didn't even cross my mind. I just watched one of the gangbangers approach Buff and without any warning, a windup, a step, a twist of the body, punch Buff square in the side of the face.

Buff didn't make a sound. His knees buckled. He looked down. The side of his face was red. But he didn't whimper or cry. When the kid who punched Buff turned, I saw that it was Junebug, the kid Buff had claimed was his cousin, the ugly kid.

They tore our house apart. They kicked in the flimsy walls. I hadn't realized how weak the structure actually was. We'd sat in the house during rain, but we'd never have survived any kind of strong wind. It was only a matter of time.

I was dragged across the roof, handed down the air-conditioning ducts. Once on the ground I heard sirens, saw the flashing lights of ambulances and fire trucks. Police officers were pulling up. They saw Buff and me being led down the street in opposite directions. They saw that we'd been roughed over, beaten. They didn't stop any of the gangbangers to ask questions. We were on our own then, and for a split second I had a flashback to when Buff had first suggested that we could build a house, a flashback to when I'd first called up to Buff, "*Hey, how'd you get up there?*" And, as I was presented to my father and yanked by my collar into the house, I longed for that feeling again. The feeling that I was all alone, that I was entirely free.

I've had other moments, since then. When I graduated college, for about five seconds I felt free. Or when I rode my first motorcycle down the alley behind my house, for about ten seconds I felt free. Then I realized I had to turn. But up there on the roof, when I was alone with Buff, I knew it, that it was all us; our lives were what we made of them. Never again have I felt as free as I did then.

Years after the pierogi factory incident I heard that Buff had been shot dead. This was in high school, my sophomore year. I was hanging out with friends in Barrett Park, where we played ball and drank beer. Ramiro said it. He always had the neighborhood news: "Hey, did you guys hear Buffster from the Latin Counts got killed? A drive-by, bro, right there on Wood Street. Got blasted in the head. Dead on arrival."

"You mean bald-headed Buff?" I asked. "Short guy, blue eyes?"

"Yeah," Ramiro said. "You knew him?"

"Yeah," I said. "We grew up together."

"No you didn't, bullshitter," Alex, another in our group, said.

"No, I did," I told them. "One summer me and him, we built a house. Over there on top of the old pierogi factory. You should've seen it. We were going to live there."

CHILDHOOD

I grew up on Eighteenth Street and Throop, in the heart of Chicago. To the east, beyond the Dan Ryan Expressway, beyond the steeple of Providence of God Church, and beyond the no-man's land that was the "darkside," a stretch of neighborhood laced with forgotten Illinois-Continental railroad tracks and collapsing smokestacks, a place said to be inhabited by the most ruthless Mexican street gang in Chicago, the Villa Lobos, was the lake. To the north were the Puerto Ricans, who were rumored to surpass the Villa Lobos in ruthlessness, said to be willing to shoot you in front of a church or in front of family, sins the Mexican gangs swore against. And then beyond them, farther north, were the whites, in a dreamland accessible only by the Chicago L, and even at that a place you glimpsed momentarily—redbrick houses, wrought-iron fences, tree-lined streets—then left, swallowed by the subway if you were on the Douglas-Park B, or forced to watch it all fade from view if you rode the elevated Ravenswood A.

The blacks were to the south. They were unfathomable. Things we didn't understand went on down there. Killings were indiscriminate. And to the west was the sunset, that's all I ever knew about the west, when evening would come and the sun would hit that point at the horizon where it flared up the long neon glass corridor of Eighteenth Street as if each *panaderia*, taco joint, and tavern had caught fire. Then, minutes later, the miracle would disappear, and up and down Eighteenth Street the kids who had lined up for blocks were left to wonder if the sun's sole purpose was to torture them with a paradise they would never reach.

We called this the Revelation. We'd named the event as kids, when Rogelio Ramirez, who grew up with the rest of us on Throop Street, began reading the Bible and reciting from the Book of Revelation as the sun set. He'd stand on the corner stoop of Trebol's tavern, Bible open in his left hand, drawing exclamation points in the air with his right. "The Woman and the Dragon!" Rogelio would say. "The Fall of Babylon!" Occasionally, the men going into the tavern would stop and listen, as if contemplating the passages Rogelio read, but something in them always snapped, and they'd break into laughter and call Rogelio "The Pope" or "The Saint of Throop Street." Rogelio never cared. He'd simply raise his voice even higher, bring his arm down even harder. Eventually, the men would retreat into the smoky darkness of Trebol's, the thick black door sweeping shut behind them. The small diamond of mirrored glass at its center staring down at us as if a horde of curious drunks were peering out from behind it. When the sun dropped below the horizon, Rogelio would snap his Bible shut, turn on his heels, and march back down Throop Street, like a leader into flames.

When we were in the sixth grade, Rogelio's mother began sleeping with Rowdy, an old Racine-Boy who lived above Sergio and Jorge Naveretté, two brothers in our group and expert spies who had devised an ingenious method by which to hear the sex going on above them.

"Check it out, bro," Sergio said the morning after he revealed the secret to me. He turned and began walking up his apartment building's stairs. That morning I had met him early for school, looking to hear Ms. Ramirez's lovemaking for myself.

Sergio stepped into his living room, past his kitchen whose boiling pots of water always made that side of the house seem more like a rainforest than a place where people lived and ate. He led me around the corner into the small bedroom he shared with his brother. There on the bed, lying on his side, was Jorge, holding a long row of paper-towel rolls taped end-to-end to his ear. The other end was up on the ceiling, inserted through a hole for a missing light fixture.

"Jorge," Sergio said. "Let Jesse see." Jorge's eyes were closed, his eyebrows raised in soft arches. He was ten at the time, a year younger than Sergio and me, but with his head to the side, his eyes closed the way they were, he seemed even younger, like the Christmas ornaments my mother had of baby angels sleeping.

"Jorge," Sergio said again. And Jorge opened his eyes but made no move to get up. Instead, he continued to listen to the cardboard contraption, alternating his gaze between our faces as if what he saw was beyond us, beyond the walls of the tiny bedroom he and his brother shared.

"Jorge!" Sergio said again. And Jorge snapped out of whatever spell he was under. He leaped from the bed. "Damn, bro!" he said.

"They're doing it doggie-style!" He sounded out of breath, excited. I took the tube and nodded, knowing from the *Penthouse*s Sergio and Jorge kept beneath their dresser exactly what "doggie-style" was.

On the other side of the small apartment, amid the cloud of humidity I had seen swirling when I passed, were Sergio and Jorge's parents. Though I lived just across the street, I had really seen Sergio and Jorge's parents only twice in my life, once at our confirmation, at our grammar school, Providence of God, and once when a disgruntled former tenant set their apartment building on fire. Otherwise their parents hardly seemed to exist at all, disappearing into doorways, driving off in their green pickup, always slipping just out of view. Whenever I walked into Sergio and Jorge's apartment and saw the swirling steam of their kitchen, I wondered if their parents were actually in there, or if they hid from their children the way they seemed to hide from everyone else.

Love affairs were a fact of life in my neighborhood. What Ms. Ramirez was doing was not that extraordinary. Stories abounded of mothers who had left their families to live with truck drivers from Texas or journeyman housepainters. And Mr. Gomez, downstairs in my building, had been seeing a barmaid at Trebol's tavern for years. Everyone knew about it, knew Mrs. Gomez knew about it. She would send her youngest son, Peter, to fetch his father from the barmaid's apartment atop the tavern. No one ever said anything.

But Ms. Ramirez was religious. Her husband had left her the year before and she had turned to the church, Rogelio in tow. When the Virgin Mary processions came singing up the street, carting the porcelain three-foot statue of *La Virgen* to the sin-afflicted apartments of the neighborhood, Ms. Ramirez was in the lead. She had inherited from the most devout before her the task of deciding how long the Virgin was to sit in the various accursed households; sometimes it stayed for weeks on end. And behind her, carrying the candles and crucifixes of the procession, the fifteen or so other neighborhood women followed like apostles. They had all lost something—sons to drive-bys, unwed daughters to pregnancies and flight-of-fancy elopements—but Ms. Ramirez had lost a husband. And though the list of things-to-weather went on for miles in my neighborhood, deserting husbands sat at the top.

"All right," Jorge instructed. "Now push it up till you hit the floor." I raised my head as Jorge worked the other end of the tube deeper into the hole. Sprinkles of dry plaster cascaded down upon the side of my face, into my eye, as I held the tube to my ear. Abruptly the tube hit flush. Sergio and Jorge looked to me. I wasn't sure what to listen for. What did doggie-style sound like? Then, without warning, unmistakable sounds began pouring down the tube. I heard the squeak of old bedsprings. I heard the scrape of bedposts against wood flooring. Most remarkable of all, I heard the voice of Rogelio's mother, who just the day before had asked me how I was doing in school but who was now moaning out "*Rowdy*," softly, quietly, as if sorry for something, grateful for something else.

I looked to Sergio.

"I told you, bro!" he said. "I told you she was up there!" I didn't say a word. Instead, I listened more closely, able now to pick up even fainter sounds, the rocking of an off-kilter night table, the groans of Rowdy himself, whose voice here was smooth and easy, different from when he was out front drinking, cursing in ways we remembered and used on our own.

I couldn't tell whether they were doing it doggie-style or any style. I only pictured in motion the *Penthouse* scenes Sergio had begun flashing before me like cue cards. I closed my eyes.

The heaves of Rogelio's mother began closing in on each other. The groans of Rowdy got louder. I imagined Ms. Ramirez sweating, her mouth open, her tongue pushed against her upper teeth like the women in the magazines. I imagined her nude but for the red heels she often wore to work. And in my imagination her shoes glowed red, radiating as if with heat in the steam-filled room.

"*Ohh*," Ms. Ramirez suddenly gasped. I opened my eyes.

"Let me see!" Sergio said. I didn't respond. Sergio put his magazine on the dresser and sat next to me. He placed his ear close to mine at the end of the tube. On my right side, Jorge did the same, a triangle of eavesdroppers.

"All right," Sergio said. "He's about to climax."

And then there was a quick trade of punches. Ms. Ramirez called out to God; Rowdy grunted; the rocking turned to a rumble, the scrapes to digs. Then there was a yell, and in that split second Rowdy's voice was thick and heavy, the way it sounded out front when he called someone a *punk-ass motherfucker* and was about to prove it. Silence followed, then a soft thump. I held tight to the tube, listening for any aftermath. Sergio rose from the bed and bowed like a matador to the four corners of the tiny bedroom. Jorge whistled softly in applause.

"Man," Sergio said as we walked to the corner of Eighteenth and Throop, our notebooks in hand, "they were all over today. Usually they're just quiet."

"Must've been horny," I said. "She always yell for God like that?"

"All the time," Sergio said. "She's going to hell." He blessed himself and laughed.

At the corner Jorge took a seat on Trebol's stoop as Sergio and I looked up the block for Rogelio and Marcitos. Up and down Eighteenth Street, the morning delivery trucks worked their horns to announce their backing into docks. The early mist had not yet burned off the neighborhood. The smell of yesterday's fried food, tacos, *gorditas*, *chicharon*, hung in the air. Soon the sun would burn the haze away and allow a fresh day's worth of fried-food smell to settle over the neighborhood. Up the block, Rogelio and Marcitos came out of their buildings. Marcitos, carrying a single spiral note-book like the rest of us; Rogelio, carrying his books and Bible in a small brown briefcase. Marcitos crossed Throop and met Rogelio. They approached us.

Providence was marooned on the darkside, forgotten among abandoned factories, outmoded railroad lines, and dilapidated wood-frame houses. I'm sure those in the neighborhood who didn't know Providence of God was back there—it was small, like any other three-flat—wondered every morning where all the kids were going, disappearing into the maze of decaying brick buildings, following the train tracks as if we were ghosts of a life that might once have existed there. We even felt like ghosts sometimes, in the winter, when the sound of our footsteps was muffled by snow, when even our breathing seemed swallowed by the thick air. In the spring, when it rained, we huddled beneath the train docks and examined the vast innards of the factories—the huge chutes that hung like descending missile silos, the conveyers that led off into distances we never had guts enough to explore. When the rain stopped, we crossed back over the railroad lines and became real again, our walks like transformations.

"Hey, bro," Sergio said as Rogelio passed us, assuming his usual position at the head of the pack. "Your mom leave for work early this morning?"

I cringed.

"She goes to work early now," Rogelio said, not turning around to look, his briefcase bouncing off his skinny leg. "I told you last week." Behind us Jorge and Marcitos, who were the same age, settled into their morning discussion about the previous day's episode of *Spectreman*. Marcitos still had a black-and-white TV and it was Jorge's duty to update him on anything he might have missed.

His blood is blue, bro. Everyone knows that.

For real, damn, I thought I saw some orange coming through.

Sergio stroked his chin.

"She must like working, huh?" he asked. Sergio elbowed me in the arm. Rogelio didn't answer.

We neared Saint Procopius, our school's competing parish. Morning sunlight exploded through the church, casting the reds and blues of the stained-glass windows onto the sidewalk below. As Rogelio passed the front doors, he blessed himself, forming a cross with his thumb and forefinger and tracing miniature crucifixes on his forehead, mouth, and chest. He kissed his thumb to heaven. In imitation, we all did the same.

"Hey," Sergio said. "How about if your mother was seeing some other guy?"

"She wouldn't see another guy," Rogelio said. "She's got the Lord." He raised a finger to heaven.

"I know, I know," Sergio said. "Everyone's got the Lord, but say you found out she was with some other guy. Maybe you came home and found her on the floor, maybe in bed—" Sergio was looking to the sky, imagining scenarios, sexual positions. He didn't see Rogelio whirl around, his briefcase flaring out at his side.

"Don't talk about my mother!" Rogelio said. He pointed a finger in Sergio's face. "Don't talk about things you don't know about." Rogelio was much shorter and skinnier than Sergio, but he held his finger right off the tip of Sergio's nose. Sergio didn't move. Rogelio turned and began walking again.

"Damn, cuz," Sergio called out after Rogelio. "Don't worry about me. I know what *I'm* talking about." Rogelio simply continued walking.

Sergio laughed and brushed himself off. He blessed himself, held up a cross of forefingers, then marched forward.

We turned down Sangamon Street. Sets of railroad tracks, the dividing line between the darkside and the realside, ran down the center. More kids had begun filling in our side of the sidewalk, all of us waiting until we got to Eighteenth Place, the street our school was on, to cross over. Our school bully, Gustavo Rivera, a large kid with sweat glands that poured like waterfalls, walked on our side as well, torturing smaller kids with "the wedge," what he called the Saturday-afternoon-wrestling move with which he crushed tiny first-grader heads between his chunky hands.

Across the tracks, only Pepe Ordoñez, Paco Martinez, and Jeremy Witek walked the darkside. We called them the Lost Boys. They had been walking the darkside for as long as anyone could remember, breaking factory windows, smoking, spray-painting unfamiliar gang signs on the crumbling railroad docks. Rumor had it they were orphans, that they lived among the ruins of the dark-side like animals, like the Villa Lobos, who for some reason, maybe respect, never seemed to mind the Lost Boys on their territory. The Lost Boys were eighth-graders. They had been held back two years or more and were actually old enough to be in high school.

"I heard Paco and Pepe were in the Audy Home for stealing cars," Marcitos said from behind us. "That they got butt-raped in there and that's why they went crazy."

"Who told you that?" Sergio asked.

"Mona Colón, downstairs," Marcitos said. Mona was a high-school girl who lived beneath him, one whom we collectively lusted after because at her age she didn't seem that far out of reach. Paco was said to have gone out with Mona. Some even said that he had had sex with her. And at the time this seemed to have something to do with his ability to walk the darkside. We figured Jeremy and Pepe had had sex with Mona as well, or with the other high-school girls who stood on the corners smoking cigarettes, wearing tight black pants and thick black eyeliner and purple lipstick. The older we got, the more we wanted to be with them, have them hanging off our shoulders the way girlfriends in our neighborhood did. We imagined French-kissing them among the collapsed rafters of the burned-out factories we had always been so afraid of.

The three Lost Boys mounted an abandoned train dock and climbed through a half-fallen brick wall into one of the factories. Up and down Sangamon Street, the kids of Providence looked on in wonder, except for Rogelio, who walked with tunnel vision a half block ahead of us, and Gustavo Rivera, who reached for the head of another unsuspecting first-grader.

At Eighteenth Place, we crossed over the tracks, walked one more block in total silence, then went our separate ways, Marcitos and Jorge to their fifth-grade classroom, Sergio and I to the sixth, and Rogelio to the sacristy of Providence of God Church, where he took prayer sessions before the beginning of every school day.

There had been a time before the Revelation readings, before Ms. Ramirez led processions, before the briefcase, when Rogelio was one of us. Back then his father was still around, and on our way home from school we would see him on the corner sometimes, talking with his partners. Rogelio would run up to him like a good son and his father would pick him up and whirl him around like a good father. Then he'd give Rogelio money and we'd cross the street to Paul's Drug Store, where we'd buy Slim Jims and Cokes, which we then consumed on the broken concrete steps of the Dvorak Park public pool, pretending we were rich, smoking thin cigars, downing dark champagne.

We only ever knew his father from these scenes and the few things Rogelio had told us—how his father was rich, owned oil wells in Texas, had stock in Shell Oil. We all lied about our families. Sergio said his father was a millionaire cattle breeder in Mexico. I said my family had houses in California, that we could see the Hollywood sign from our backyards, some with better views of the sign than others. After hearing Rogelio's lie, Sergio began telling kids at school that his father had stock in Shell Oil too. In the court-yard, when the girls asked me or Rogelio if what Sergio said was true, we always said it was, that all three of our fathers had stock in Shell Oil, that our families were part owners and that we all split profits. When asked why we weren't living in the mansions we claimed to have, we pounded our chests the way the gangbangers did and claimed it was the neighborhood. That we had family here, even the people we didn't like. And those listening always nodded in understanding.

Those days were full of talk. Talk about our favorite team, the Chicago White Sox, and the hated Chicago Cubs. Talk about where we wanted to visit when we got older: Alaska, Yellowstone Park, places we had researched in our school's only set of encyclopedias, which were guarded by our school's secretary, Ms. Margaret, in the main office. We talked about running away. Rogelio had mentioned his aunt who lived in Aurora. Aurora sounded like a nice place and I told Rogelio if he wanted to go I would go with him. Sergio laughed at us for thinking we would ever run away, and when we thought about it more, we knew he was right, and became embarrassed for thinking so childishly.

But Rogelio changed after his father left. In the beginning it was just the Revelation readings, which were fun because for a while we thought Rogelio was joking, the way he wrinkled his brow, the way he moved his arm stiff and strong. But then he started going to church even on Saturdays, our baseball days, our football days. He had become an altar boy and had to stay after school for practice. In the mornings he stopped going straight to class and instead showed up somewhere around third period, having missed most of the morning praying back in the sacristy. And finally, when we did talk to him, Rogelio talked about things we didn't care about, religious things: *You know that Brother Adam went to Providence when it was all Polish?* Little by little Rogelio became someone else, someone we didn't know except for what we remembered.

We continued listening to Rogelio's mother. I showed up at my usual time two days later and found Marcitos there. Sergio had obviously passed word. We divided up the half hour between the four of us, Jorge keeping time on his father's silver watch. At one point, Ms. Ramirez said, "I love you." Marcitos was listening.

"She just said, 'I-love-you,'" Marcitos said, inflecting the couple's rhythm.

"Let-me-hear," Sergio said. And they talked like that the rest of the morning. Even to Rogelio, who had become remarkably more distant in the past few days, walking even farther ahead of us, sometimes leaving us altogether.

"Your-mo-ther-still-lea-ving-ear-ly?" Sergio asked as we walked to school.

Rogelio said nothing.

"Hey," I called out to Rogelio. "Remember they used to call you the Pope? Remember we were going to run away?"

Rogelio didn't answer. When he passed the doors of Saint Procopius, he blessed himself. In routine, though we were a full city block behind him, we all did the same.

A week later I showed up at Sergio and Jorge's building and found the front door open. Upstairs, their apartment door was open as well. I stepped in and tiptoed through the creaky living room, past the dripping kitchen. I opened the door to Sergio and Jorge's room and saw the usuals, Jorge with the watch, Marcitos sitting on the bed, and Sergio with his stack of magazines. But there were three new kids there as well, one with the tube, now bent and velvety, to his ear, and the others on either side of him, watching Sergio flash his *Penthouse* scenes. I recognized one of the new kids from Morgan Street, a side street we often used on our way home from school. I hadn't seen him since months before, but his face, especially his eyebrows, which were upturned in a perpetual scowl, had stuck with me as a mark of a person to avoid.

Sergio continued turning pages. "This is Carlos," he whispered to me, nodding toward the kid with the tube. "And Joseph and Tony." He took a breath. *"I think I'm going to start charging."* He whispered this even quieter. He smiled and gave me a nod like I should agree with him.

"Jesse," I said, introducing myself to Joseph and Tony. I skipped over the kid with the tube. Tony, the kid I remembered, pounded his fist to his chest two times as I shook his hand. It was *Amor*, insider gangbanger stuff, done to represent a Nation. Rowdy pounded his chest when he said what's up to people. He was an old Racine-Boy. But Tony did it obviously, because he was a Morgan-Boy, or if he wasn't, an older brother was.

"Are they doing it doggie-style?" I asked Carlos.

Carlos opened his eyes, his head still sideways. "How should I know?" he said. And those in the room began laughing.

We took turns. Two minutes each. Jorge keeping track on his father's Timex.

We went through the order and the tube finally came to me. Ms. Ramirez and Rowdy were talking. I was trying to pick up their whispers, searching for the words I thought people in love might say—*love, babies, marriage*—but in the crowded bedroom, concentration was difficult. I breathed, put my hand over my open ear, closed my eyes. Still, I heard only the heavy rush of silence, and an occasional echo too distorted to be understood.

"*Se fue la Virgen!*" somebody cried in Sergio's gangway. "*Dios mio!*" A door slammed. The sound of footsteps could be heard between buildings. Sergio stepped to the side window, saving with a finger his place in the *Penthouse* he was working on. I handed the tube to Tony and went to the window as well. Jorge and Marcitos followed.

Mrs. Gonzalez, the woman who lived in the downstairs apartment, was running up the narrow gangway, yelling that the Virgin had flown away. She turned the corner onto the sidewalk and the three of us shuffled around the end of the bed to the front window. When we arrived, Mrs. Gonzalez's blue shawl was fluttering out of range. We turned for the living room, where two more windows looked upon the street. Sergio flung his *Penthouse* onto the bed. Carlos, Joseph, and Tony stayed with the tube.

As we rushed through the bedroom door, Sergio suddenly stopped in his tracks. We stacked up behind each other, my chin jabbing into Sergio's shoulder and Jorge's chin into mine. Standing in the sun, at the living room windows, were Sergio and Jorge's parents. For the first time ever, I saw them up close. At our confirmation, and the time their building had been set on fire, their father had worn a baseball cap. Now he wore no hat at all, and I could see that he was not only bald down the center of his head but that his scalp glowed a bright scarlet like he had some kind of infection. His belly bulged within an old cowboy shirt and his arms seemed longer than they should've been: his wrists were visible beyond his shirt cuffs. Their mother stepped closer to us, taking tiny steps, and it occurred to me suddenly that the mother and father were complete opposites. While the father was lanky and bulbous around the waist, the mother was short and compact, muscular looking in the thick brown sweater she wore. She had a full head of gray hair pulled back in a tight braid, like something you might see on a young girl.

"*Que estan haciendo?*" she asked. When she opened her mouth, silver crowns on her bottom row of teeth caught light. She looked past us through the doorway and into the bedroom. Tony and Joseph still had their ears to the tube. Carlos had his eyes on the watch. Sergio's magazine was strewn across the bed, its wrinkled and worn centerfold opened up and in clear view.

Her backhand rose like a reflex. It was so fast I felt its breeze as it whizzed past my nose and cracked Sergio square across the left side of his face. Sergio reeled back, bringing up his hands to shield himself. I stepped aside and his mother landed two more smacks, more dense-sounding, to the back of Sergio's head.

She whirled around, her stiff braid unmoving. "*Salganse de mí casa!*" she screamed at the three on the bed. Carlos, Joseph, and Tony rose like soldiers, abandoning the tube still wedged in the ceiling, leaving the silver watch lying on the bed. As they passed through the bedroom door they brushed up against the doorjamb, eying the trigger hand of Sergio's mother.

She turned to me and Marcitos and pointed her short, wrinkled finger in our faces. She told us she was going to have a long talk with our mothers, then stared at us with her flared-up eyes like miniature Revelations. "*Sacanse de aquí,*" she said to us, and we followed her finger as it turned toward the front door. "*Largense a la escuela!*" As I stepped into the hallway I saw, through the corner of my eye,

Sergio's father, his scarlet patch boiling, closing in on Sergio and Jorge.

A small crowd had assembled on the front stoop. Mrs. Gonzalez's daughters, Vilma and Louísa, who already looked like their mother, old and bowlegged, though they were our age, were out there telling Carlos, Joseph, and Tony that during the night the Virgin had disappeared. That they had had it for the past week, trying to sober up their father, and that when they had awoken, the Virgin was gone, the window she had been placed by opened. Their mother, they said, had gone to get Ms. Ramirez up the block.

"She's upstairs with that guy," Tony said.

"Who?" said Vilma, stepping closer to Tony.

"Ms. Ramirez, that lady who leads the processions, she's upstairs with that old Racine-Boy."

"Ms. Ramirez is up there, Jesse?" Louísa asked me. She grabbed my arm and pulled me close, mashing her thick, immature chest against my arm.

"I don't know," I said. I worked my arm free.

"Is it Ms. Ramirez?" Louísa asked, and she stepped close to me again. "Is Sergio up there listening?"

"Not anymore," I said. She latched onto my arm. Tony and the others laughed. I looked up the street for Rogelio and Mrs. Gonzalez.

Neighbors were out by this time: Pedro, who lived in the other downstairs apartment, just home from his third shift at Ryerson steel, his brown skin coated with a white powder that made you wonder exactly what he did. Bernardo Ruiz, in a metallic-blue housecoat, who lived the next building over and danced evocatively during all the block parties, who everyone knew was gay but who never found trouble for it because he was ours, a member of our block, our gang, was there as well. And some of the more astute procession ladies had arrived also, their pink and green hair curlers seeming to have picked up the potential for controversy like radar. The Gonzalez daughters began calling up the stairwell to Rowdy.

"Rowdy," Vilma said. "Is Ms. Ramirez up there?"

"*Tenemos un* emergency," Louísa added.

I looked for Rogelio again. I figured he would be able to calm everybody down, convince Mrs. Gonzalez that the Virgin hadn't actually flown away, that someone had simply stolen her, and that, besides, the Virgin was only a statue anyway, and another could be bought at Opal's Ocultos on Eighteenth Street. But I also knew Rogelio's mother would be coming down the stairs any minute, that Rogelio would see her and realize we had been up there spying.

By now Sergio, Jorge, and their parents were downstairs, their father with his cap on. Sergio's face was flush, his eyes glazed over. Jorge, on the other hand, seemed content, as if things, at least for him, could've gone worse.

"What's going on?" Sergio asked softly.

I told him about the Virgin. I told him how Mrs. Gonzalez was trying to find Rogelio's mother. He looked up the stairs and whispered, "El trutho comes outo." He rubbed his hands together and smiled. For Rogelio, I nearly punched him.

Mrs. Gonzalez finally came waddling back up Throop Street. The procession regulars from Rogelio's building followed. She came to us, her lips trembling. She held her fingers to her mouth. Just as she took a breath to speak, a step sounded, and we all turned to look up the apartment building's stairs, to where Ms. Ramirez in her red pumps had appeared.

She came down slowly, each step accompanied by the sharp clap of a heel on the hollow wood stairs. She held onto the doorjamb as she stepped over the threshold. She stood on the building's concrete stoop and scanned the small crowd.

"Don't look at me like that," she said to everyone. Her voice was crisp and sharp. She had no makeup on. Her skin was darker than usual, her lips pale. She was pretty. She turned to the procession ladies. "I'm sorry, all right," she said, leaning forward. "But I'm not like you. I don't want to be lonely." On the first-floor landing Rowdy was standing, only his hairy legs and white boxers visible.

Ms. Ramirez stepped from the stoop and walked through the crowd. She looked to me. I could tell she was upset but I knew she wasn't upset with me. I looked into her eyes and knew she had no idea I'd been up there listening to her make love to Rowdy.

"Where's Rogelio?" I asked her.

"Rogelio?" she said. "He left. He didn't tell you?"

"No," I said.

"He went to stay with his aunt, yesterday. He didn't tell you?"

"No," I said.

"Sorry," his mother answered. "I'll tell him you asked." She turned up Throop Street and began walking toward Eighteenth Street. The seam of her tan skirt was just off-center, making it seem like there was a limp in her step. The crowd turned to look up the stairs, but Rowdy was gone. Within the building a door slammed. The sound echoed through the halls and exited the open windows. The old ladies started in.

"*Sin vergüenza!* What are we going to do now? Where's the Virgin?"

No one knew what to do about the Virgin. Mrs. Gonzalez was assured by Sergio and Jorge's parents that it hadn't flown away, although Tony, the Morgan-Boy, kept saying that it had. That maybe the sin of the Gonzalez household had been too much for the Virgin and that she had flown back to heaven.

"Sin overload," Tony said. He sighed and shook his head. Mrs. Gonzalez began to cry.

That incident brought an end to the Virgin Mary processions. No new leader came forward. The apostles seemed uninterested in electing anyone.

I fully expected to see Rogelio again, as if he had only gone away on vacation. But a couple months later his mother moved out of the neighborhood as well, she and Rowdy loading up a rickety-looking U-Haul, a puff of black exhaust hanging over the corner of Eighteenth and Throop like a final farewell.

I don't know if Rogelio found out we were listening. I sometimes think he did, and that that's why he left. But then again maybe he didn't. In some ways I feel like he vanished, was stolen, kidnapped, like the Virgin out of Mrs. Gonzalez's window. I know he wasn't. I know his mother probably met up with him in Aurora and that they settled there, or somewhere else, maybe even farther away, a different state. Maybe he still remembers how it was when we were young. When childhood was the only neighborhood we lived in.

SNAKE DANCE

CLIMBERS

They waved to each other like peeping toms. They had half smiles on their faces, unsure if they were happy to be seen—to be discovered meant the roof they were on, the perch they were on, was no longer sacred. The next day someone else was sure to be up there, potato-chip bags, coke cans, candy wrappers scattered carelessly like a slap in the face.

Some were hyper-secretive. When they were spotted atop a church steeple or warehouse roof, they scattered like mice. If there was nothing to hide behind, like at the top of one of the abandoned water towers, they raced back and forth like the Marx Brothers until it occurred to them that they could be out of sight on the opposite side. If you followed them around they kept themselves just out of view, like squirrels being chased up a tree, until eventually they stopped, and tried to blend in as much as possible with their surroundings.

Other climbers were proud, walking the edges of A-frame roofs, the ledges of dilapidated apartment complexes. They did tricks sometimes, like gymnasts on the balance beam, flipping and doing graceful cartwheels into dismounts where they arched their backs and threw up their hands in pride. They did this during rush hour, when even the side streets were packed with commuters searching for easier routes home. "Gapers' block" it was called, when a car would stop, nearly causing an accident, to see a kid doing pommel-horse maneuvers atop the old pierogi factory on Oakley Avenue.

And some kids were sitters, thinkers. They sat and contemplated life, the state of the world, on the various roofs and ledges of the neighborhood. A subspecies of the sitter was the painter, who could be seen, sketchbook in hand, legs crossed, back stiff, painting skylines from various vantage points in the city. Sometimes there were schools of them, small herds who sat together and painted in much the same style, watercolor, surrealist, even Gothic—adding buttresses to the Sears Tower, complicated barrels and pinnacles that connected all the buildings downtown as if it were one large medieval complex. If you watched them long enough, you'd eventually see them turn to each other, give a smile, take a breath, shake their drawing hands for just a second, then jut their chins out and continue again, legs crossed, backs stiff as boards.

Then there were the subterraneans. Those who did their exploring, their investigating, underground, in the dark beneath the sidewalks. They wore flashlights attached to various parts of their bodies: foreheads, arms, legs. They looked like monsters, lit-up monsters, as they made their way through the caverns beneath the city: the old coal railways, the ancient pedways beneath the Loop.

They knew the city's complex system of tunnels like they knew the wrinkles in the palms of their hands. They were able to follow each tunnel, see where it was going, all this in advance, as if they were viewing it from above.

They initiated new members with a turn at the lead, telling them to simply calm down if they felt lost, because a true spelunker has this "sixth" sense. "Remember," they said, "you always know where you are, always." And they were always right.

From time to time a spelunker would pop up out of nowhere, through a basement door, coal hatchway, chimney flue, or in the subbasement of an L station or tavern. "Excuse me," he would ask of anyone in sight. "Do you happen to know the time?" And the spelunker would wait, patiently, sweaty, his face covered in grime. Behind him, the flashing yellow lights of companions could be seen, small talk could be heard: "The best way is under Ogden Avenue, by far. Maybe Pershing as an alternate."

"What about Archer?"

"Ends at Western."

"Aaaah."

The stunned civilian would check his watch and reply and the spelunker would always ask, "A.m. or p.m.?"

"Thanks," the spelunker would say, when he had his answer.

"Eleven o'clock, boys," he would say as he was turning. "*A.m.!*" And a small cheer would go up as the spelunker would shut whatever grate or door or wooden trap he'd come from, and disappear.

I remember these characters as if they still run through my life. I remember these characters like I saw them just yesterday, scurrying across the L tracks or down into a deep gangway. They were all so shy, so secretive, but when you saw them they'd salute, smile, just a little happy that they'd been seen.

DISTANCE

C hano says he's never seen the wall open, but I know it's a lie. It's one of those things you never pay attention to, it happens so many times, like the sunrise, or a freight train running across your neighborhood. I pay attention when I see the wall open. You see things out there, the horizon, tiny stone islands like miniature castles. "Water-pumping stations," the professor says. "Not castles. We don't have castles where we live."

The professor tells me the wall was first built to keep the Indians out, then the Russians. He throws up his hands. "It's a relic," he says. "A piece of machinery left over from an age of fear, fright. Things are different now." Still, the wall stays closed, except to let the ships in. Those we sit and watch.

We walk along the piers with the professor. He is old and decrepit, so he has to hold on to my shoulder. The others walk ahead. Chano, Sylvia, Suzie. I can hear them talk, sometimes about girls, boys, sometimes about movies. Sometimes they make fun of me, call me an old man. They turn around and giggle. Mostly, though, I pay attention to the professor.

"All the time we used to go up there," he says, looking to where the pedways used to span over our heads. "We used to fish and swim down here on the docks, then walk up the ramps just to sit. We'd watch the sun travel across the sky. We'd see birds, peregrine falcons, hawks. Sometimes they'd swoop down and pluck a fish from the lake with those huge talons. Ah," the professor says. "It's great to see birds in the distance."

I look to the abutments, the ramps leading to nothing, and try to imagine bridges, pedways, crisscrossing over my head, the view that must have been afforded. All that's left now are the rebar innards of the reinforced concrete, which bristle from the ends of the abutments like things to hold on to when you're falling over a cliff. Layers of multicolored graffiti cover the walls, and from one abutment a lone metal handrail just out of scavengers' reach dangles and reflects the sun.

I seem to have a memory of looking over the wall. I seem to have a memory of watching the sunrise, seeing the pastel pink-and-blue shades of the horizon. I have a memory of fins in water, dolphins or sharks. And I have a memory of birds gliding, sometimes diving steep, bombing dives, and pulling up large flopping fish, only to lose them as they tried to carry them away.

DAMASCUS

"In Damascus they wear long robes. In Damascus they have white, pointy beards and they all look like the guy from Hills Bros. drinking a big cup of coffee.

"In Damascus they cut off your hand if you steal something. They blind you if you look at another man's wife. They cut out your tongue if you tell a lie.

"In Damascus there are people with milky gray eyes who can see into the future, and you can sit by them in the marketplace during your lunch break and ask what crimes you will commit.

"In Damascus the fortune-tellers are walled in by carpets, tall, bright carpets that vendors hang on high rods. Everywhere you turn there is a wall of carpet, and it makes you think of flying carpets, like you can pull one down, start it up, and fly away.

"In Damascus the women hide their beauty. If they are married, they wear long black sheets; if they are engaged, they wear light blue; and if they are neither married nor engaged, if they are old maids, they just wear plain white. You never see their faces in Damascus. In Damascus the only things you see on women are their eyes, dark and Chinese-looking, and this is what men fall in love with, eyes. See, this is how Damascus is different.

"And they have camels. In Damascus they have many, many camels. And the camels crowd the marketplace, chewing their gums like old men, like Willy who sells the newspapers on Leavitt Street. And they smoke, oh do they smoke—the people, not the camels— they smoke night and day, like crazy. At any time you can smell the cigarettes, burning, rich and powerful, like a fog, sweet and damp. And they sit in their doorways, the people. They sit beneath their arched doorways that lead into their deep, dark apartments, and they smoke, exhaling thick exhaust into the tiny, twisted streets.

"In Damascus, when the sun goes down, all you see are shadows. Those buildings with the arched doorways, those that are built tight into each other, those buildings that form the streets, twisting and turning—at night, in Damascus, those buildings become lit from the inside, and crescent-moon-shaped windows, star-shaped windows, cast patterns on the white walls of the buildings across the way. In Damascus at night, no one speaks, and if anyone walks, his footsteps can be heard echoing down the corridors of street, scraping and shuffling. And the streets are so narrow that someone walking miles away can be heard just as clear as someone right around the corner.

"See, this is how it is in Damascus. I know. I have been there."

SNAKE DANCE

Papo stepped to the DJ. He cocked his arm. He had that flair in his eyes. The same flair I had seen hundreds of times when Papo was drunk and he was about to kick someone's ass. I held Papo back. I don't know where I had him, maybe I just pushed back on his chest. I could feel Papo's arms—that's it, I had him by one arm. When I pushed back I had his biceps in my hand, in my palm, his long, thin biceps, like Bruce Lee's biceps, defined, like the contours of the fenders he Bondoed together when we crashed our cars. Papo was a mechanic.

"What are you, a fucking Indian?" Papo said over my shoulder. I took a quick glance behind me, at the DJ, hoping he wouldn't say anything back. I'd analyzed the situation. I'd anticipated everything. When the DJ showed up, I took a look at him, judged him: *Goatee, a little chubby, doesn't look like he'd start a fight, doesn't look like he'd back down. He won't get drunk.* I looked at the DJ again, there, later, made eye contact with him, right after Papo asked him if he was a *fucking Indian.* I saw a smile, a placating smile, a back-down smile, an "I don't want any trouble" smile, a "But why do you think I'm an Indian?" smile. I wondered the same thing. *Where did Papo get that?*

"It's all right, Papo," I told him.

"But he's not doing it right."

"What?" I asked him. I could still feel his biceps. He was still straining. The fibers of his muscle were fine and hard. "He's not doing what right?"

"*La vibora*, the snake dance, he's supposed to do it right after the dollar dance."

"It's all right," I told Papo.

"No, bro, it's your wedding. He's supposed to do the snake dance. *Fucking Indian*," he said to the DJ, this time louder. I could hear the clink of beer bottles. Someone was tapping on the side of a glass with a knife, *kiss the bride*, they were saying. This was a Mexican wedding. I didn't know where my wife was.

I turned around and looked at the DJ. "It's okay," I told him. "Just go on with the dance music." The DJ nodded.

I gently pushed Papo back toward the tables, toward the bar packed with people I hadn't seen in years, friends I'd felt obligated to invite, people I could never not love.

"I just want it to be right," Papo said. It sounded as if he was about to cry. I thought of Papo's little girl, Crystal, his wife, Bernadette, who'd left him two years before, the cocaine habit that had him running to the restroom every hour, the .25 automatic he kept tucked under the armrest of his Cadillac Brougham.

"I want it to be right for you," he said.

Papo turned and headed toward the bar. I put my arm around his shoulder.

"It is right, bro," I told him. "It is right."

Hours later I was in the banquet hall parking lot saying my last goodbyes. Most of the party guests had left, my in-laws, my father, my uncles. Only Papo was there, in the dim light of the streetlamps, and two other friends, Danny Boy and Mario, friends from many years past. Just to my left, sitting in the passenger seat of the car I had rented, was my wife. I could see her silhouette, the outline of her hair, the white shoulder of her wedding dress. I was anxious to leave, to start my new life.

"Go be fucking married, then," Papo said. He was smiling, he shook my hand. "Good luck," Mario said. Danny Boy gave me a hug like I was leaving forever.

"Go be fucking married, then," Papo said, this time a little louder. "Motherfucker."

He was standing behind me. I could feel him there. I could see him out of the corner of my eye. I turned to look.

Danny Boy pulled at Papo's arm.

"Mother*fucker*!" Papo said. He stepped toward me.

Mario got in front of Papo.

"Just go, bro," Danny said.

"*Motherfucker!*"

I climbed into the rental car and shut the door. I could smell my wife. All night she had smelled beautiful.

"What was that?" she asked me.

"That was Papo," I answered.

In the rearview mirror Danny Boy and Mario were struggling to hold Papo back. I turned onto Damen Avenue. The three of them started fighting, there in an empty parking lot, on the South Side of Chicago.

MAXIMILIAN

I want to tell you three memories of my cousin Maximilian. Two of them involve his fists.

My cousin was a short man. He was, however, like everyone else on the Mexican side of my family, built like a brick two-flat. Maximilian was heavy and hard. He was a cannonball, the way my grandmother on my mother's side was a cannonball, the way my uncle Blas was a cannonball. They were all skull, they were impossible to hug, but they were warm-blooded, steaming, like just standing next to them could get you through a winter's day. My mother was like this. I miss her terribly.

But Max, my cousin, *Maximilian*, was young. He was sixteen or so when my memories of him first begin. It was at his sister Irene's cotillion, in the basement of Saint Procopius church on Eighteenth Street and Allport. I don't know much about the planning. I was eight years old. But I know my sister, Delia, stood up in it. She was a *dama*, and my cousin on my father's side, Little David, was her *chambelán*. They were off doing their own thing, dancing, waltzing, the way they had been practicing for weeks, my sister constantly fitting and refitting her dress, me calling her Miss Piggy because she was chubby and more *queda* than the rest of us darkies.

That night I sat with my mother and ate cake and people-watched. My father, done with his shift at the basement door, was at a side table sharing a bottle of Presidente with his friend Moe. My cousin Chefa was dancing with my uncle Bernardo. My aunt Lola was on the floor dancing with her only son, my cousin Maximilian. The music fit the moment, *balladas*, slow, sentimental. It was all beautiful, all quite nice. Then Stoney showed up.

I am not sure my uncle Blas would've allowed any boyfriend of Irene's to attend the cotillion, but Stoney didn't have a chance. He had issues, most noticeably the tattoo on his neck that said ALMIGHTY AMBROSE.

No one had been at the door, not at that moment. So Stoney and his four partners simply burst into the basement. They had to be high. My father and Moe walked up to the four. There was wrestling, chair throwing, screaming. There were two gunshots, pops that sang off the basement's polished cement floor, the massive concrete support columns. Then the police showed up. Arrests were made— three paddy wagons' worth. But the moment I remember most, right before my mother pulled me under the table, was catching sight of my cousin Max, on his knees, his fist jackhammering over and over straight down into Stoney's limp head. I couldn't see Maximilian's face, his head was bowed, but I could see his thick shoulders, his biceps bulging within his dress shirt. Behind him my aunt Lola was pulling at Irene, my uncle Bernardo was reaching for Max, and my father had one of the gangbangers up by his collar. All of them were staring down at Max. All of them had looks of horror.

Maximilian ruptured something. His arm and fist were in a cast for months. I don't know what got worked out, but Irene kept seeing Stoney. Eventually they married. Stoney never had a cross word for Max, not that I ever heard.

Memory number two happens a few years later, when I was eleven. By that time Maximilian was eighteen and he had just graduated from Juarez High School. He had joined the army and we were having a going-away party for him in the yard behind his father's house.

I had lived in this house, back when my parents were split up over my father's cheating. I had spent nearly a whole summer there, holidays included. I had my own bed, the bunk over Maximilian's. Where other houses were hard to find, my uncle Blas's house was simply forgotten. The Kennedy Expressway rumbled within yards of the back door. Out the front door the South Branch of the Chicago River turned. There were neighbors to either side, but still my uncle's house was lost.

His party was a year or two after I had moved back in with my parents, and though I had seen Maximilian nearly every weekend since I'd left his house, at the party he seemed aged. He had grown a thin mustache. He had on shorts and a Dago-T. His muscles looked thicker than usual. His skin was dark, worn even.

Maximilian was never a big talker. But as the afternoon progressed and he continued to draw from the keg, he spoke more freely, eventually calling out my name like I was a friend of his from the street.

"Jes-se!" he would say. "I love you, bro." And then he would start laughing.

Late into the party, the adults were drunk and I remember Maximilian putting his head under the tapper and chugging beer right from the keg. He was smiling, laughing as he gulped. He came up choking, spitting suds. He stumbled around the gravel yard trying to catch his footing. He seemed momentarily blind, lost in his spinning head. We were laughing. My mother had her arm around my shoulder. My father had his arm around my uncle. When Maximilian fell on his ass we doubled over in laughter. We were roaring. And at that moment we seemed really together, my father, my mother, my aunt and uncle, my cousins Irene and Chefa, Stoney, my sister, even my cousin's dog, Princess. For a moment there, we were a real family. Behind us traffic droned on the Kennedy Expressway. And just out the front door, the South Branch flowed.

My last memory of Maximilian is from a couple of years later. I was thirteen. Maximilian was in his twenties. He was home from Germany, on leave because his mother, my aunt Lola, had died.

As sick as my aunt Lola had been, her death was mostly unexpected. In just a few weeks her cancer had gone from manageable to terminal. The last time I saw her was two days before she died. She was back in St. Luke's Hospital and when I said hi to her she could only look in my eyes. Her look scared me. It was the kind of look that needed a voice to explain itself.

My aunt Lola was a generous woman. The months I lived with her she always had a steaming bowl of *frijoles* waiting for me when

I came home from school, two or three thick tortillas waiting to be dipped and sucked from like summertime *paletas*. My aunt's most remarkable feature was her bridge, which she would pull from her mouth and set on the armrest of her La-Z-Boy as she sat and watched TV. When she dozed off I would try to put the bridge in my own mouth. As my months of living there wore on, I used to steal her bridge and move it to some other location, in her bedroom or on the kitchen table, then wait for her to wake and be forced to speak, her pink gums showing through her fingers as she asked if anyone knew where her bridge was.

Her wake was held at Zefran Funeral Home, on Damen and Twenty-Second Street. There were masses of people there, cousins I didn't know I had. Though I loved my aunt, and loved the *frijoles* she used to leave me, at the wake I felt no need to cry. Flowers were placed on her chest, blessings delivered to her open casket. At one point a boy standing next to me, a boy who had been introduced to me as my cousin, began to cry. He turned and gave me a hug. I wasn't sure what to do. So I patted his back. "I know," I said to him. "She was a good woman." The kid raised his head and looked at me like I was at the wrong wake.

After the viewing we packed into cars and lined up for the funeral. The procession was long, too long for our family. My uncle and his daughters were behind the hearse, riding with my father in his black, windowless work van. A few cars back, Maximilian and I rode alone in his Chevy Celebrity.

We were silent as we drove down Pershing Road. Maximilian had placed our orange FUNERAL sticker on the top of the passenger-side windshield, and for me it was like a sun visor even though the day was overcast. The tick of the Celebrity's hazards matched our engine speed, lagging as we braked, then racing when we sped to catch the car in front.

At Oak Park Avenue we slowed for a red light. Our hazards were on. Our orange sticker displayed. We followed the car in front of us into the intersection. Suddenly a red pickup took off from the crosswalk. The pickup broke through the procession just in front of us, then continued south down Oak Park. There was a short pause. Long enough for me to consider what an asshole the pickup driver was for cutting off the procession. We were on our way to a funeral. I had that much in my head when Max threw the Celebrity into a left-hand turn so sharp my temple knocked against the passenger-side window.

We chased the truck for three blocks, the Celebrity's hazards clacking so loud they seemed about to explode right through the dash. Finally the driver of the pickup pulled to the curb.

Through the rear window of the cab I could see the man jerking around. He looked out of his mind, yelling to himself. As we pulled up behind him his shoulder heaved and he threw the truck into park. His taillights flashed to full red. He kicked open his door.

We were in front of a bank parking lot. It was the middle of the day but the lot was empty. Black screens covered the plateglass windows as if the bank was closed for good. Trees lined the street. I felt a million miles from home.

The truck driver slammed his door shut as Maximilian was stepping out of the Celebrity. The truck driver yelled something. He was a big man, white, potbellied. He was wearing a flannel shirt. His neck seemed like one big chin and his jeans seemed too tight at the waist.

Each one of his steps had a little bounce to it, as if he had learned to walk on his toes.

The man continued yelling as Max moved forward. Maximilian didn't say a word. He simply continued to close in, his feet looking small, his shoulders broad, his tight waist neat with his tucked-in dress shirt. His tie was draped over his shoulder.

As Max got within arm's reach the truck driver raised his hand and pointed to my cousin's face. The man's mouth was still going. He was looking down at my cousin. He was giving him a deep, mean look, eyebrows pointed in, teeth showing as he screamed. I think he thought Max was going to stop and start yelling himself. Max simply kept on moving, and just as the man was ending a word, drawing his mouth shut, my cousin lit into him with a flush right hand that sent the man staggering backward. Even in the car, over the now practically dead heartbeat of the blinkers, I heard something snap, the man's jaw, his neck, my cousin's wrist. The man fell to a seated position and Maximilian bent over him and hit him three more times, solid, deep-looking punches to the left side of the man's face. The man fell sideways and was out cold. His short arm flopped over his thick side and landed palm up on the street. Maximilian turned and started walking back to the car. His face was red now, swollen. He was crying. He looked like he wanted to yell, to scream, but couldn't get anything out. The Celebrity's hazards had stopped dead. The car had died. I wished we were back in the procession. I wished there was somewhere, anywhere, for us to go.

GOD'S COUNTRY

Ask him where he learned to do that stuff and he'd say, "Sonora, God's Country." Chuey had never been to Sonora. He spent every day of his life right there in Pilsen, just like the rest of us, playing ball, jumping the freights. We thought maybe he'd resurrected some witch doctor's memories of being in Sonora. I mean, he resurrected everything else: dead cats, dogs, finally a human being. So when people asked us how he learned to do the things he did, we said, "He learned it all in Sonora, God's Country." There seemed to be no other explanation.

He was fifteen when he found out he had the gift of life. It was one of those mornings we skipped school. It was early, right around the end of first period.

"Poor fucks," Alfonzo said, looking to the high school, the kids transferring classes. "I'd be in algebra right now."

"English," I said.

"I'd be in gym," Marcus said.

"*Booo*," me and Alfonzo answered.

"No, man," Marcus said. "Gym this early is a drag. All sweaty afterward. All sweaty for Brenda Gamino second period."

"Damn," Alfonzo said. "You have Brenda Gamino in a class?"

"Second period," Marcus said. "History." He pulled out the joint he had in the inside pocket of his leather. We were standing in front of the Pilsen YMCA, just across the street from Juarez High School.

"We're going to get busted," Alfonzo said. He said this as a matter of fact. That year, our freshman year, we'd been caught skipping three times by December. The limit was five unexcused absences per year. Our parents had been called. We'd been reasoned with by Mr. Sanchez, the school social worker: "So if you get expelled, what kind of job are you going to get?" We didn't know. We didn't care. The only thing that seemed to matter was that the thought of school made us literally, physically ill.

Marcus pulled out his tiny Bic lighter. He lit the joint and took a deep, early-morning drag. He passed the joint to Chuey, who hadn't said a word all morning. Marcus exhaled.

"Want to walk to Speedy's?" he asked.

Collectively, we began to move.

It was cold out that day. Alfonzo and I had on our hooded sweatshirts. Marcus had on his black leather. Chuey had on that brown, crusty leather jacket he always wore, the same one he had worn all summer. An *heirloom* he had called it that first day he showed up with it on. "It was my great-grandfather's."

"Looks like it," Alfonzo had said.

"The fuck's an heirloom?" Marcus asked.

"Something special," Chuey said.

For weeks after that everything was an heirloom, a quarter someone had for a video game, a last piece of gum, a last cigarette in a pack. Some people called them "luckies." We called them heirlooms. "I only got one left, that's my heirloom," we'd say. Chuey just continued to wear the jacket.

We walked down Twenty-First Place. The street was empty. All the factory workers had left for work, all the cleaning ladies, the secretaries, had taken their L's downtown. Twenty-First Place was the only street in our neighborhood that had any trees, tall, full trees that lined the sidewalk for exactly two blocks. On summer days Twenty-First Place smelled good, fresh; birds sang and fluttered in the branches. Out of habit, on winter days we stuck to Twenty-First Place as well, even though by that time the birds were gone, and Twenty-First Place was just like any other street, cold and gray.

We kept our hands stuffed deep in our pockets, reaching out only to toke and pass the reefer. As we neared the corner of Paulina Street a beat-up white Cadillac pulled around the corner. The car jerked to a stop, seesawing in the middle of the intersection. Heavy bass rattled the trunk lid. The four of us stood still, ready to bolt down a gangway, jump fences. At the rear window a hand came up and rubbed out a hole in the steamed-over glass. Someone peered through, directly at us. Then the hand came up again, this time wiping with a blue piece of sleeve. The person looked through. We saw the face, dark, thick eyebrows, wide, flat nose. The person smiled, then held up the Almighty Ambrose hand sign. Then the car took off, tires screeching, tailpipe sparking as it knocked against the uneven street.

"Capone," Marcus said.

"I know," Alfonzo said. We all knew. Capone was someone we could recognize from a block away. Pilsen seemed like it would be a better place if he'd never been born.

Capone was an addict. He did everything: coke, heroin, happy stick. His favorite pastime was cornering kids in gangways. "What you be about?" he'd demand, a crazy, mindless look in his eyes. "*Am-brose Love*," the kids would stammer out. They all knew the routine. Capone liked to bum cigarettes. When taking one he'd say, "Let me get a few more for later." If you protested he'd say, "Want to fight about it?"

One time he asked Chuey for a cigarette and Chuey said no. Capone punched him so hard in the chest that Chuey lost his breath. There should've been payback. Chuey's family were all Two-Ones. Chuey could've said something and all four of his brothers, a few uncles even, would've been out hunting for Capone—and they would've found him. But Chuey never said anything. "It doesn't matter," Chuey said. "It's not like that fucker will ever learn." Chuey was right. Once or twice a year Capone was beaten, bloodshot eyes, cut-up face, casts over broken limbs; even looking like that he'd be out gangbanging. Still, it would have been sweet to know Capone's ass had been kicked yet again, and that Chuey's brothers had done it.

"Just remember that car," I said.

The Cadillac peeled off onto Twenty-Second Street.

"If they come back around we'll meet up behind the Farmfoods."

We continued walking.

We passed the old funeral parlor, the large, arched doorway that was once the entrance to a barn at the back of the building. We passed beneath the stone horse's head, the words FUNERAL PARLOUR embedded in color tiles in the arch. Now the building was just another place to live, like so many other storefronts in our neighborhood, boarded-up plateglass windows, marquees covered with plywood, everything washed in a deep maroon as if to match the dirty brick of the neighborhood.

We turned north and headed toward Speedy's corner store. Our joint was running short. Chuey passed what was left to Marcus. "We should get some more weed," Marcus said. He pinched the lit joint and brought it to his puckered lips.

Chuey took a breath.

"I can bring things back to life," he said.

I turned.

"What did you say?"

"I can bring things back to life," he said again. "I did it this morning, a dead bird."

Chuey was staring down at the sidewalk. His hair hung low over his brow. His arms were locked at the elbows, his hands in the pockets of his jeans.

Alfonzo and Marcus turned.

Marcus was trying to position the roach in his fingers.

"You can bring things back to life?" Alfonzo said.

"Yeah," Chuey said. He lifted his head. He gave a jerk to get the hair out of his eyes. "I don't know how. It was an accident. I was walking by Wolcott and I saw this thing in the alley. It was green, a parrot, with a red beak."

"We don't have parrots," Marcus said. "Too cold."

"I know," Chuey said. "That's why it was weird. Then I went over there and just touched it. And the thing woke up and flew away."

I wondered if Chuey had been smoking earlier. He did that sometimes, got high alone. I looked at his eyes. They weren't glossy like they usually were when he smoked too much. They weren't lit-up either, as if he might be telling a joke. But then Chuey wasn't one to tell jokes. Generally what he said was serious—even if it was funny, like a story, it was always true.

"Maybe the bird just got knocked out," I said. "They fly into windows and shit."

Chuey shrugged.

"Why would you touch a dead bird, anyway?" Alfonzo asked.

"For real," Marcus said. "That's fucking gross."

"Show us where you found it," I said. And Chuey took the lead. He headed down Cullerton Avenue. We were high. At that point we really started to be high. For some reason I remember snow falling, but I don't remember any snow being on the ground. In any case, things suddenly seemed to be happening, more things than I could register, and all I recall about the rest of that day is the burnt-orange leather of Chuey's jacket, and Chuey talking fast and pointing things out in the middle of an alley.

Chuey was a hippie; at least that's what everybody in school called him. I'm not sure they even knew what a hippie was. Chuey was more a rocker. He'd introduced us to Rush, Pink Floyd, Led Zeppelin. Chuey gave us our first taste of reefer, back in the seventh grade—he'd stolen it from his cousin Rom. Even then everyone called Chuey a hippy, *we* called Chuey a hippy, but back then it was because of those crazy shoes he wore. He didn't start wearing that funky leather jacket until high school.

White-boy shoes, that's what they were. Black, brushed suede. None of us would've dared to wear such things. They were Herman Munster boots, and if it wasn't for Chuey's long brown hair we might have called him Herman Munster instead of Hippie. Herman Munster or White Boy, one of the two. Chuey never tied his boots. They looked like they would get left behind if he ever had to run anywhere. Of course, Chuey never ran anywhere. Which was one of the reasons we hung around with him. We never ran anywhere, either, spending our lunches instead on the Thomas Cooper Elementary School steps, trying to look cool for the girls, trying to believe we were anywhere but school, trying to ignore the fact that a school bell dictated our lives so completely.

By high school, though, Chuey had adopted at least part of the Pilsen uniform: black Converse All Stars. He still wore straight-leg jeans. The rest of us wore Bogarts—baggy pants with sixteen pleats cascading from the waist, tight cuffs at the ankles. It was strange that Chuey didn't adopt more of the neighborhood style. He had grown up in Pilsen, just like the rest of us. In fact, Chuey's roots were deeper in the neighborhood than any of ours were. Our parents had come straight from Mexico. Marcus, Alfonzo, and I were first-generations. Our parents worked in factories, didn't speak English. Chuey's parents were gangbangers, old gangbangers, sons and daughters of immigrants. Chuey seemed a step ahead. Like if we ever had kids they'd come out like Chuey, a little more worldly than we ever were. We were jealous of Chuey for who his family was, people who had tattoos, people who had served time in jail, men with names like Hustler, Shyster, Red, women named Chachie or Birdie. These were the people a child growing up in Pilsen heard stories about, people who gave someone from our neighborhood life, history. Chuey never seemed to care. He didn't walk with pimp. He didn't magic-marker gang initials on the white soles of his Converses. He didn't tattoo things on the backs of his hands. Rather, Chuey just seemed to be drifting.

Two days after that day in the alley we were sitting in the school atrium. We were smoking Alfonzo's Kools. We were not high.

"I did it again," Chuey whispered.

We were on lunch.

"Hey, bro," Alfonzo said. "Aren't you supposed to be in biology or something?"

"Yeah, I know," Chuey said. He was still whispering. "But listen, I did it again."

"What?" Alfonzo asked.

"Raised the dead, bro," Chuey said. He was excited, smiling. "Another bird, man, a little sparrow, right outside my window. It must've froze to death."

I looked to the group of girls sitting behind us. They had heard Chuey. They were laughing, making faces. I smiled at them.

"I asked my great-grandfather," Chuey said. "He said I had the gift of his people, the Seri, back in Sonora, God's Country." By now the girls behind us were paying even more attention. I pinched my fingers and touched them to my lips. The girls started laughing again.

"You're not an Indian, bro," Marcus said.

"No, but I have the gift," Chuey said. "It's in my blood."

None of us said anything.

Chuey's great-grandfather *was* an Indian. Back in grammar school we once sent Chuey home with phrases to translate. The next day he came back with these crazy sounds that were supposed to be words: "*Motherfucker* is..." "*Give me a beer* is..." "*Hey baby what's your name* is..." The language had hard *t*'s and heaves yet still managed to sound somehow Spanish. Chuey's great-grandfather still lived in Mexico. He sent Chuey things: that ugly leather jacket, a rusting metal pendant, a small sack of tin coins. It was junk, the stuff you'd find in a secondhand store on Eighteenth Street. Chuey called them heirlooms.

"We can go after school," Chuey said to us.

By this time the girls behind us had returned to their own conversations.

"Go where?" I asked him.

"To find dead things," Chuey said. And then he walked away.

After school that day we hit the three places we thought most promising: the alleys behind Martin's hot-dog stand, Del Rey tortillas, and Slotkowski sausage. Each time there was nothing, not a dead rat, dead bird, or dead cat to be found.

"Just our luck," Alfonzo said. "When you need a dead animal you can't fucking find one."

"No shit," Marcus said. He tilted back a garbage can. "I thought the city was putting rat poison down. There should be a shitload of dead rats."

"They're probably immune," I said. "Super rats." I peeked down a long, descending gangway.

"Hey, bro," Alfonzo said. "Does your magic work on trees?"

"I don't know," Chuey said.

"They're dead, right?" Alfonzo asked. "In the winter."

"No," I said. "I think they're just sleeping."

"We should try it," Marcus said. "Maybe it'll work."

So we walked back to school, back to Twenty-First Place. After a short search we found the tree that looked the most dead: twisted branches, peeling bark, white streaks down the trunk like the tree had been bleeding. Above us the streetlights were just flickering on. The sky had a dark lavender color.

Chuey took off his jacket.

"Does it hurt?" Alfonzo asked.

"No," Chuey said. "It's weird. I don't even feel anything. But I know it's coming so it almost hurts."

Chuey took a deep breath. "Ready?" he asked.

We all nodded.

Chuey reached out and tapped the tree. He did it quickly, as if expecting an electric shock.

We waited.

We waited even longer.

There was nothing. No sudden blossoms, no thick, heavy leaves, no fresh bark climbing up the diseased-looking trunk.

"Touch it again," Alfonzo said.

"No," Chuey said. "This is not how it works. This is not what it's meant for."

"Well, it's getting fucking cold out here," Marcus said. He blew into his hands.

We started to move toward home.

Twenty-First Place was flooded with orange street light now. Tree branches cast long shadows against the two- and three-flats. In the sidewalk, messages etched before the cement had dried stood out like miniature mountain ranges: PARTY BOY LOVE, MARIA-L'S-FRIDO 4-NOW.

We crossed an alley. I took a quick glance down to the other end. There, in the middle of the alley, resting in the shallow drainage canal, was a large black mound.

"Look," I said.

"Damn," Alfonzo said.

"If that's a rat..." Marcus said.

We walked down the alley. As we got closer the mound began to take shape: a fat pink tail, a wide belly, yellow teeth propping up a long, pointy head. It was the biggest rat any of us had ever seen.

"That fucker's huge," Alfonzo said.

I picked up a rock and threw it. I hit the rat square in the ribs. Nothing.

Alfonzo stomped on the ground. He waved his arms over his head. Still nothing.

It was the size of a small dog. The tail alone was so fat that wrinkles were visible, fingerprints, almost.

"You sure that's not an o-possum?" Alfonzo asked.

"What the fuck's an o-possum?" Marcus said.

"Just like a rat, only bigger. They got them in Jew-town, by Maxwell Street."

"That's a rat, man," I said. I looked down to the animal, its stiff, short hair. I gave the body a kick. The entire thing moved, a block of ice. Even the tail held its stiff s shape.

"You're going to touch *that*?" Alfonzo asked Chuey.

Chuey didn't answer. He got down on his knees and started to rub his hands together.

"Those things got diseases," Marcus said.

"Shhh," I told Marcus.

"Those things can jump too," Marcus said. "One time, in my gangway..."

"Shut up, asshole," Alfonzo said. He yanked back on Marcus's hoodie. They both fell in behind Chuey.

Chuey pushed the sleeves of his brown jacket up to his elbows.

I scanned the porches of the apartment buildings around us. In some windows Christmas lights had been hung, tight crisscrossing patterns, steep triangles. In a few windows the designs had collapsed, leaving only sagging, drooping strings of lights, barely hanging on, like a wino's pants. Through some windows blue TV reflections could be seen, brilliant flashes against white plaster ceilings, Christmas specials probably, *Miracle on 34th Street*, *It's a Wonderful Life*. At that moment the whole city seemed asleep.

Chuey blew into his hands. He took a deep breath and closed his eyes. After a moment he opened them. Then he reached out and stabbed with his finger at the rat's hind leg. We waited. I looked to Alfonzo. Beneath the powerful alley lamp his breath was luminescent. I looked to Marcus. He was on his tiptoes, trying to see over Alfonzo's shoulder. Nothing seemed to be happening.

"There!" Chuey said. "There it is!" Down on the concrete the rat's large body began to move.

That night, in that alley, we witnessed creation, maybe re-creation. Life came to the rat in a wave that spread from the hind leg, where

Chuey had touched it, to the front and rear of the rat's body. The tail whipped. The front legs jerked and twitched. At the head, the rat's mouth clapped shut. The rat thawed before our eyes: its belly dropped; its back arched; its hair stood on end. There were no flashes, no sparks, just the rat heaving, then breathing, then darting for the nearest bank of garbage cans. We jumped and screamed. We yelled for Marcus, who had run to the end of the alley. We hugged Chuey. He had the gift of life.

Those months we missed a ton of school. First there were the pigeons kids would shoot from their apartment-building windows. Then there were the stray cats the Ambrose tortured and left hanging from alley light poles. Then there were the puppies left in cardboard boxes, dumped in empty lots. Really, there was so much to do.

At first we experimented. Did the power work best at night or during the day? Did Chuey always have the gift or did it flicker in and out, off and on, like the *W* in the Woolworth's sign over on Twenty-Second Street? As it turned out, the power was always on. Chuey could raise the dead whenever he wanted. Only time of day seemed to make a difference, and that affected only speed. Early mornings a cat would come back in a matter a seconds. Later at night it seemed as if the power had drained slightly. Things came back reluctantly. The process even appeared to hurt a little.

Within a couple of weeks we had a set routine. I was security. I made sure there were no witnesses, gave a whistle if someone was coming. Marcus tended to the animal, herding it in the safest direction once it came back. And Alfonzo, who had been an altar boy for two weeks back in the sixth grade, gave the invocation.

"May the holy ghost follow you through your new life. May you hold dear this blessing from God's Country."

Chuey did the work.

Besides us, only Chuey's great-grandfather knew what we were doing. Since the discovery he'd become a coach, instructing us on how to use the power. "Ask him if we can bring back humans," Marcus once told Chuey. "We could go to Graceland and bring back Elvis."

The following day Chuey had a response. "My great-grandfather says the power is to be respected. It can be used only for the common good." His great-grandfather's answers always begged more questions. Eventually we stopped asking things altogether.

We met under the trees on Twenty-First Place. From there we combed the streets. After the streets were cleared, we moved on to garbage cans, where we found parakeet mummies wrapped in newspaper, cloudy-eyed goldfish wrapped in toilet paper. The goldfish we collected in a Tupperware dish Alfonzo had stolen from his mother's kitchen. Then we took the fish back to Marcus's house and gave them life in the warmth of his basement bedroom. By late February Marcus had more fish than he had space for, and we started calling him Aquaman and telling him he was going to grow gills. Every time we found a new fish Marcus would say, "Hey, you guys need to take some." But we always protested and said our parents wouldn't let us.

We all started collecting things. Alfonzo had a puppy he'd named Cloudy. We'd found Cloudy frozen behind the junkyard on Peoria Street. His legs were stiff. His white coat was matted and ugly, bald in some spots. When Cloudy came back his coat was fresh and new, thin and wispy. We could feel Cloudy's ribs as we held him up and had him lick our faces. He was a puppy again.

By March I had three birds: a finch named Ron Kittle, and two parakeets—Harold Baines and Mike Squires, my White Sox all-stars. I had found a birdcage in the dumpster behind my apartment building; I began calling the cage my dugout. I was anxious to add Carlton Fisk to it.

By late March, by spring, all four of us had maxed out on absences. Our parents were called in. We made excuses. I claimed that gangbangers were after me, that they had threatened to kill me unless I joined their gang. Mr. Stoner, the disciplinarian, asked me to name names, and I rattled off a few I had seen spray-painted on our neighborhood's walls. Tom Cat, Jerry Mouse, Player, Jouster. My parents were sympathetic. So was Mr. Stoner. He let us all stay in school with promises that we would not miss another day. We even signed contracts. By April, though, we were missing days again, and by May, by graduation, we had stopped going completely.

Those days were fun. It seemed quite possible that we could make careers out of raising the dead. We could leave the neighborhood, travel the world, resurrect important figures in history. Already I found myself scanning the obituary pages of the *Sun-Times*, cutting out clippings of former presidents, kings and queens, rock stars, anyone famous, creating a list of important people we had to bring back to life. We wondered together if there was a statute of limitations on Chuey's power. Could we bring back Martin Luther King Jr.? Could we bring back George Washington if we ever found where he was buried, or King Tut, who had been on display at the Field Museum downtown? These questions were on all our minds in late May, when Chuey told Brenda Gamino he could raise the dead.

I am not upset. The truth is Brenda could do that to a man. The second week of school I'd tried to ask her, "So how do you like high school?" Only my tongue got thick and it came out more like, "How do oh a hisco?" She just looked at me and smiled. "What?" she said. I wanted to kiss her right then and there. Her voice, even questioning me the way it was, was soft and warm. I think I wanted to marry her.

"No, no," I said. "High school... I mean... if you like it... is what..."

"What?" she asked again. And I just turned and walked away, my Adam's apple so far up my throat I felt like I was gargling.

Marcus had done it, and Alfonzo too. Brenda just made people say stupid things. But Chuey had been saved. He was too embarrassed. He'd never said a word to Brenda. I believed Chuey when he said that *Brenda* had been the one to start talking to *him*. Her question had been, "What are you going to do this summer?" And in the heat of the moment, in the desperate search to say something of meaning, something she would remember, Chuey replied, "Raise the dead."

She didn't mind us much, Brenda. I'm not sure she remembered that any of us had ever tried to talk to her. Those last few weeks of school we used to pick her up, the four of us. They weren't really even dating, not yet. They would walk together, laugh out loud, hold hands. Marcus, Alfonzo, and I would follow, smoking cigarettes, anxious to get back to the business of Life, hoping someone like Capone didn't show up to make us look stupid.

Brenda used to say things: "You know, they're not going to let you guys back in." "We know," we would reply. "We have a plan." But her comments began to have an effect. More and more while out on rounds, Chuey would start talking about going back to school, going to summer school even. Our plans were at risk.

So maybe he showed her at some point. Maybe they were walking after a rain and he found a dead worm on the school baseball field. Or maybe they found a dead bird, a pigeon hit by a bus, or a sparrow who'd ingested rat poison. Chuey said he never showed her, that he never even brought up the power, but he must've done something—otherwise she would've thought he was crazy, talking about "raising the dead" the way he did. But maybe she thought he was a little off anyway. When you're a teenager you're willing to take more things on faith. Reality hasn't been defined by experience. Anyway, she asked Chuey, the night her brother OD'd, to bring him back to life. And then Chuey called us, and at 11:30 p.m., May 15, we met at Twenty-First Place and started walking to Brenda's house. The trees were in full bloom by then. Even at night the smell was like inhaling through a sheet of fabric softener.

We didn't know Brenda's family. Chuey didn't know them, and he'd walked Brenda home dozens of times. It's no wonder, though, that she kept her family a secret. I wouldn't have admitted to Capone either.

It's beyond me how they came from the same family. One of them must've been adopted. Brenda looked like her mother. They had the same eyes. But then Capone had their mother's skin—dark, sandy. So who knows, maybe they had different fathers. For so long Brenda had seemed otherworldly—even with her talking to Chuey, she was still beyond us, beyond Marcus, Alfonzo, and me. Yet here she was, sister to the most obnoxious gangbanger in Pilsen. Things suddenly seemed possible.

He'd OD'd in his bedroom. Brenda walked us there after meeting us on the sidewalk. They lived in the back basement of a narrow three-flat. Their apartment was cool and wet; the concrete floor was glossy with humidity. Carpets covered some spots and as we walked through I found myself taking long strides from carpet to carpet.

Capone was sitting on the floor, leaned up against his bed. His head was cocked sideways, his chin dug into his chest. White vomit streaked down the left side of his mouth onto his black T-shirt. He was filthy. He stank. He looked like he hadn't bathed in a week.

"How long has he been this way?" Marcus asked.

"We just found him," she said. "Maybe a half hour ago."

"No, dirty like that," Marcus said. "When's the last time he took a bath?"

"*Que dijo?*" their mother asked.

Brenda ignored her.

"I don't know," Brenda said. "He leaves home for weeks, then just shows up for breakfast or something. We haven't seen him for a month."

Her mother looked to us like she was waiting for a response.

The last time the four of us had seen Capone was back in the winter, back when that white Cadillac had stopped in the middle of Paulina Street. I wondered if he'd been stoned since then. I wondered if his death was the end of a five-month-long high.

"You sure he's dead?" Alfonzo asked.

"His heart's not beating," Brenda said. She raised her eyebrows like Alfonzo was an idiot.

Alfonzo nodded in return.

Chuey got down on a knee and reached for Capone's wrist. He searched for a pulse, using two fingers, stopping at various points like he knew exactly what he was doing.

Capone's arms were covered in tattoos. On his right forearm, close to his elbow, were the masks of comedy and tragedy, both crying large white tears. Just below was a fat, green, faded crucifix. And then at his wrist, where Chuey was searching, the word AMOR was written in Old English script.

"Can you do something, Jesse?" Brenda asked. She used Chuey's real name. No one ever used Chuey's real name, not even his family. I wanted to correct her.

Chuey sighed. "An hour max," he said. "Easy death, no violence. We'll take care of it."

I looked to Alfonzo and Marcus. They both looked at me. Chuey had never sounded so official.

Chuey reached into his pocket and pulled out a penlight. He pried open one of Capone's eyelids and then shined the light in. He pulled the light away and brought it back quickly. He did this two or three times for each eye. With each flash he gave a small grunt as if whatever he was looking for wasn't there.

Capone's pants were stiff and crusty. They were blue but hazy, spotted with dirt and grease. They looked like the pants of an alley auto mechanic. Capone's socks had been white at some point. Now they were black at the soles, lighter shades of gray toward his ankles. I couldn't believe Capone was on the floor, dead. I felt a sense of satisfaction. I felt like cursing him, talking to the dead body, making up for all those times he'd hassled me on the streets of our neighborhood. *Serves you right, motherfucker.* I felt like kicking him.

Chuey continued with his examination. He wiped Capone's chin and neck with an edge of bedsheet, then felt under Capone's jaw the way a doctor does, lightly, gently.

I thought to remind Chuey of that time Capone had punched him in the chest. I thought to remind Chuey of what he'd said back then: "*It's not like that fucker will ever learn.*" Then suddenly I remembered what Chuey's great-grandfather had said way back in January, how the power was to be respected, how it could be used only for the common good. We weren't *supposed* to bring Capone back. Our job was to bring back harmless things, cats, birds, dogs, goldfish, a decent human being—not Capone. I opened my mouth to say something, but then I saw Chuey look up to Brenda. He smiled and nodded with confidence, reassurance. He was going to bring Capone back, common good or not.

"*Qué van hacer con mi niño?*" Brenda's mother asked.

"Mom," Brenda answered in English. "Just let him be. He knows what he's doing."

On a bedside table a burnt-out glass tube sat looking like it was about to roll off and shatter on the concrete floor. In the center of the table a tiny Bic lighter, blue, just like the one Marcus carried, was standing upright.

"You guys let him smoke in here?" Alfonzo asked.

"He just does it," Brenda said. "I tell her all the time." She turned to her mother. "But she won't just kick him out." She said this last piece forcefully. Her mother didn't bother to look.

"We're going to have to lay him down," I said to Chuey.

Chuey gave a nod.

"They like to kick," Marcus said to Brenda. He smiled like an apology.

I reached down and started to pull at Capone's arm. The closer I got the more I picked up his odor. He was sour. I didn't know if it was the drugs, the death, the filth, or all of the above. Alfonzo and Marcus went for Capone's legs. I could see the looks on their faces as they pulled at his ankles.

Chuey was on his knees. He started to rub his hands together.

"*Qué van hacer?*" Brenda's mother asked.

"It's okay, *Señora*," I said to her. "*Somos professionales.*"

She was holding her hand up near her mouth. She was leaning to one side, watching us, waiting for what we were going to do next.

"Okay," Marcus said. "Ready." He grabbed Capone's left leg. Alfonzo grabbed the right.

Chuey was breathing deep now. His eyes were closed. He looked like he was preparing for a dive, like I'd seen competition divers do once on a National Geographic special. Then he started humming.

Brenda's mother turned to her.

"*Mom*," Brenda said. "He's an Indian. This is a ritual."

I rolled my eyes.

"Does anyone else know we're here?" I asked Brenda.

"No," Brenda said.

"You didn't call the police?" I asked.

"No," she said again. "We found him and I just called Jesse. I know what you guys do for a living."

There was a pause. Even Chuey stopped humming. I expected

him to open his eyes, to look at me, to us, for our reaction. He began humming again.

"What's his name?" Alfonzo asked Brenda.

"Leo," she responded.

And then, as I waited for Chuey to give his gift, for some reason I began to feel close to Capone. I'd seen him around for so many years, spoken to him so often, said *what's up* in hopes of avoiding confrontation. I'd even run from him a couple of times, when my appeals to his human side failed. As I stood there looking at his limp body, things started to make sense. I could see him growing up in the tiny basement apartment. I could see him in Cooper Elementary, where I had gone. I could see him making friends, hanging out with the Latin Ambrose, until suddenly, almost unexpectedly, he couldn't turn back. I felt sure Capone was a father. Maybe his girlfriend was one of the young mothers, the gangbanger girls I'd seen walking their babies on Saturday afternoons. I looked to his mother. She was old and tired, like my mother, like all our mothers. She still had her hand up near her mouth, hiding it, as if her lips might reveal more than she wanted to. Without me realizing it, Capone began to seem normal. I felt like we were all in the same boat, like our neighborhood, Pilsen, was just a rut people fell into. I began to think we were doing the right thing. That maybe Capone had seen God, or someone, or something, and was going to come back a new man, reborn. Maybe he'd seen the other side. I studied his tattoos, the upturned spear, the name CAPONE written in script on his neck, under his ear. Maybe this was what the gift was meant for, second chances, or even a chance at all.

Finally Chuey stopped humming. He opened his eyes and

nodded to Alfonzo. I tightened my grip.

"*May the holy ghost follow you through your new life,*" Alfonzo said. "*May you hold dear this blessing from God's Country.*"

And then Chuey tapped Capone's ankle.

Like always at night, it happened slow. First his right foot twitched, then his left. Then there was nothing. Seconds passed. Two or three minutes even. Then his fingers twitched. Then his whole body snapped, for just an instant, like his muscles, his veins, had suddenly inflated. Capone wheezed, a breathless, flat wheeze, barely audible, but it was noise, and Capone had made it.

"*Dios bendiga,*" Brenda's mother said. She dropped to her knees. "*Mijo!*"

Capone growled. His chest heaved. It wasn't breath—breathing hadn't started yet, but Capone's lungs swelled, then emptied. Brenda's mother reached for Capone.

"*Don't!*" Chuey barked.

Brenda's mother snapped back, startled.

Then real breath started. It was obvious. Capone's chest rose and fell, slowly at first, then quickly, then regular, like his lungs had found a rhythm, had caught up to the beating of his heart. He was mumbling, every breath seemed to carry a sentence

"*Mijo!*" his mother called out. "*Aqui estoy, mijo,*" she said.

Capone's mother reached for him again. This time Chuey let her go.

Capone opened his eyes. He stared into his mother's face. He had that wild look, the same one he had when he was high, when he was pushing kids up against walls, asking them what they "*be about*," ready to kill. His mother was whispering to him. She was returning his stare, praying for him. Then Capone flexed his arms. I felt him pull. His biceps bulged; his eyes widened. I leaned all my weight into his wrist, trying to pin it to the floor.

"It's all right!" Alfonzo said from below. "It's okay, man, relax. Leo, let it go!"

"It's all right, Leo," Brenda said. "You're home, you're here, you're safe."

Then Capone gave a cry, a shriek. Another spurt of energy shot through his arms, his body. I leaned into his wrist again. On the other side Chuey did the same. Suddenly Capone gave way. His arms went limp. His eyes went clear. Now he was Capone, Leo. Now he was alive.

"*Mamá*," he said. He was breathing hard, panting. Sweat was pouring down his face, beading up on his nose, his unshaven face.

"*Mamá!*" he cried. "*I know what I did.*" He was sobbing. "*I know what I did, Mamá.*" he said again. "*I saw the other side.*"

Capone's mother wiped his face with her bare hand. She grabbed his cheeks and kissed his lips.

I loosened my grip on Capone's arm. Chuey, Alfonzo, and Marcus released their holds as well. Capone was still. He was whimpering. Brenda got to her knees. His mother was hugging him. Then Brenda was hugging him. Then they were all crying and hugging together.

"You're okay, Leo," Brenda said to him. "You're okay."

"*I did something wrong*," Capone said. "*I know what I did. I saw myself.*"

"It's okay," Brenda said to him. "You're back now. It's over."

Capone continued to whimper. His smell was stronger. The whole bedroom smelled spoiled, like clothes that have sat in the washer too long.

"You know," Marcus said. "It's easier when we bring them back in the morning." He wiped his forehead. "They don't fight as much."

No one responded.

We waited for a long while. They wouldn't let go of each other. Finally Brenda's mother sat up. She looked to Chuey, who was sitting on the edge of Capone's bed. She turned to him and grabbed his hands. She held them close to her chest. She still had tears in her eyes. "How did you learn to do that?" she asked him. She was speaking softly, quietly. "*A donde aprendiste eso?*"

"Sonora," he said to her. "I learned it all in God's Country."

Then she smiled and kissed his knuckles.

We were on top of the world. For a while nothing could bring us down. It was a natural high. We woke up feeling powerful, breathing easy, clear. We went to sleep feeling the same. We were rejuvenated, ready to hit the streets. Alfonzo made plans for a bus trip across the country: "St. Louis," he said. "Gateway to the West." So we started collecting money; Marcus even sold some of his goldfish to the kids in his building. We were on our way somewhere, out of Pilsen. Then Chuey said the power needed a rest.

A rest was understandable. We'd been going at it since Christmas, nonstop. Maybe Chuey was getting tired. Honestly, we were getting tired as well. Capone had come at just the right time to keep us going, but when we thought about it, we needed a break too. Our vacation was to last two weeks. Middle of June we were to pick up right where we left off. We'd have more money by then. St. Louis was just around the corner.

The first day of June, Chuey started summer school. We didn't even know he'd registered. He'd signed up before the end of May, before we brought Capone back. Chuey said that he hadn't, that he'd only registered a few days ago, but this didn't make any sense. We knew he was lying.

But we came up with an alternate plan. During the week, while Chuey was in school, Marcus, Alfonzo, and I would scout bodies. We would list where things were, rank their importance. Then on the weekends Chuey would join us, give his gift. This was a silly idea—even then I knew it wouldn't work. Marcus seemed like the only one interested. I can say now, honestly, that by then Alfonzo and I were just looking for something to do. With Chuey in school our days had become just as long and boring as they were before we found out about the power.

We continued to meet under the trees on Twenty-First, only now it was just the three of us. Marcus had a little notebook where he'd jot down streets and intersections, types of bodies as we found them. After a few days even Marcus began to see the ridiculousness of what we were doing. One afternoon we found a pigeon in an alley, dead, shot, bleeding from its eye. It had fallen from the telephone wire above. An open attic window was just a few feet from the line, a straight shot with a pellet gun. Marcus crouched next to the pigeon. Then he reached out and touched it. He waited and waited. He asked Alfonzo to give the invocation. So Alfonzo did.

Marcus breathed deep and clear. He hummed with his eyes closed. And then he touched the pigeon again. Still, there was nothing. We walked in silence, split up, then went our separate ways home. That was the last day we ever went out on rounds.

A few weeks later, in early July, Alfonzo and I registered for the second half of summer school. It was a painless experience. Our social worker, Mr. Sanchez, wound up being our summer school counselor. He praised us for having "changes of heart" and then convinced us to get the hard classes out of the way first, algebra and U.S. history. Seven hours a day, a half-hour lunch, two fifteen-minute breaks. At least we were in the same classes. Marcus refused to enroll. The day we asked him, his response had been, "You know, I can't ever see myself in a classroom again." We knew he was serious.

There were changes of heart in Brenda's family as well. Capone had become a new person. He'd cleaned himself up. He'd stopped the drugs, stopped the gangbanging. The week after we brought him back to life, Brenda's mother took him shopping, and not shopping at Zemsky's Discount, or Goldblatt's, but shopping like downtown, Stacey Adams, Marshall Field's. She bought him an entirely new wardrobe, new shoes, ties that matched his socks. Brenda told us his mother would only buy him long-sleeve shirts and we knew this was true because eventually we saw Capone ourselves, walking to the Eighteenth Street L station, a brown bag lunch in his hand. He had landed a job working at a law firm downtown, shelving books. He had a tie clip, wing-tipped shoes, no earrings. At his wrists, peeking out from under his shirt cuffs, were the thick green scallops of his tattoos. At his collar, on his neck, the top edges of his name were visible. But he had a nice smile, and with him for some reason this seemed to go a long way. When he saw us he said what's up and raised his lunch bag for show. He kept walking like he was in a hurry. He gave us a smile.

That August, Capone was killed in a drive-by shooting. He had just stepped out of the Woolworth's on Twenty-Second Street. He had bought some T-shirts to wear under his dress shirts. A gang-banger, a Disciple, was walking by at the same time and someone in a passing car, aiming for the Disciple, shot Capone once in the right temple. He was dead on the scene. There was no hope. Chuey was in school.

Alfonzo and I heard the rumors. We were in school by then and we heard how someone had "paid" Capone back, and how he "got what was coming to him." The whole neighborhood knew the shot was meant for someone else, but the way rumors work, people believed what they wanted. I never said anything. I knew what we had done, that we had served the common good.

I don't know exactly what killed Chuey's power, or even if it's dead at all. Chuey is long gone. He lives up on the northside now with Brenda and their kids. With some investigation I could get Chuey's phone number—his family still lives in the neighborhood. But I'm not sure what I would ever say to him. It seems as if we've already done enough.

Like so many people from Pilsen, Marcus simply disappeared. I talked to him off and on all through high school. He was working at UPS for a while. He met a white girl there and they moved in together. Then suddenly there was nothing. He was gone, disappeared, like childhood.

Alfonzo joined the army. He lives in Arizona now and builds

helicopters. I still talk to him, once a year or so. We always remember Brenda, how she made people say stupid things, how Capone was killed just when he was getting started. Beyond that I am not sure what else we say, though our conversations sometimes last for hours.

I still live here, two blocks from where I grew up, four blocks from where we brought that first rat back so many years ago. I still think about raising the dead, every day. Sometimes, in my bathroom, I will find things, a dead spider, a dead ladybug, or, every so often, a cockroach. And just for fun I will close my eyes, open them, and touch the dead body. I'll hope that my finger will give life, that I'll feel again what I felt when I was fourteen, when, in this whole damn neighborhood, among all this concrete, all these apartment buildings, church steeples, and smoke stacks, we were somebody.

SIDE STREETS

In some quarters the death had become a macho thing. After all, the story involved Casper walking a full city block to the nearest tavern and ordering himself a beer so he could get change to call himself an ambulance. From all accounts, Casper had been shot at least three times that night.

It wasn't uncommon to see kids acting the whole thing out. One skinny brown kid running up to another and pointing a thumb and forefinger pistol at a mate's chest, then voicing three loud "booms" before skittering back to his hiding place. Here, it seems, the children always embellished slightly. The "boom" they used, as everyone knew, was reserved for imitations of a .45, and Casper had been shot with a .38. But they did it anyway, it made for more dramatics, and on side streets dramatics count for more than reality.

The child portraying the fallen hero, Casper, would usually stagger down the street, making small guttural noises as if gurgling blood. Sometimes the role player would say something like

"I have—to—get—to Trebol's, get me—some—change," but nobody knew if Casper had really muttered these words. A few stumbles usually followed. Trips over his own feet, a couple of all-out collapses, complete with the customary pre-death limb twitches. But the player would always find it in himself to rise up and get to the front door of the local tavern, where he would say, "Give me an Old Style" (the brand varied depending on the player). This was as far as the act ever went, and at this point the performance was judged.

Technique was most important—the player, through all his ad-libs and theatrics, had to convince the others that he was the actual person, had to convince unsuspecting adults that he really had been shot. It was never enough. There was always some other kid who claimed he could do it better. That he could've pulled off the act ten times better and could've fooled ten times as many people. So the play would go on, back and forth, until dinnertime, after which the act was tried out at night, when realism abounded.

More than just Casper's death marked that day twenty years ago. God knows the neighborhood crawled with death back then. Each day some new mutilation would present itself and give the church groups and the men working on their Ford pickups something to talk about. But with Casper's death an aura emerged. Even years later, each person who recounted the story did so as if the event had happened only days ago. The real good storytellers in the neighborhood claimed the scene ran through their minds like a massive car crash: everything in slow motion.

In the churches along Eighteenth Street, the mothers were reminded of Casper's death while performing their stations of the cross. They'd see the Virgin Mother embossed on those plaster moldings and imagine Delores Calderon, Casper's mother, in the Virgin's place. Delores had become a martyr, a woman who had had to give up her son for something better, and they all wanted to be like her. They all wanted sons who could take Christ's place on the plaster moldings the way they imagined Casper could.

Mostly in pity but sometimes in jealousy, the mothers lit prayer candles for Delores's and Casper's souls—one extra when the mothers were really feeling mournful, and always two or three extra on the anniversary of Casper's death. On those days, the immense light emanating from the overabundance of candles climbed the cold marble walls of the churches and shone through the stained-glass windows onto the annual memorial services held on the front steps. The light filtered out effortlessly, casting upon the crowd the soft oranges and blues of the glass mosaics.

Mrs. Calderon's disappearance wasn't all that unexpected, at least when it first happened. For the females, a period of mourning is always anticipated. For the males, on the other hand, a stout heart is required; appearance at work the next day is mandatory. Casper, though, had no father. The older women in the neighborhood said that his father had died in a steel mill before Casper was born. Whatever the case, Mrs. Calderon mourned alone. Speculation as to her whereabouts didn't start up until three weeks after Casper's death. Usually, during mourning, one is at least seen—perhaps walking, aimlessly and sorrowfully—but seen nonetheless. With Mrs. Calderon, there had been nothing.

Her apartment was broken into by the local clergy, her bank accounts traced, but all anyone could discern was that she had somehow vanished. Some said that she had gone back to Mexico to reclaim an illegitimate child. Some even believed that she had committed suicide, maybe jumped off the Twenty-Second Street bridge, where it was commonly said that "if the fall doesn't kill you, the polluted river will." Most likely, though, and a few of the older mothers knew this temptation from having lost children of their own, Mrs. Calderon had simply become a shell of a woman, and had returned to Mexico to live her final years without the constant reminder of her son's death. Still, it was an odd thought. To think that that once-strong woman, that bowlegged brute who used to waddle down Eighteenth Street carrying bags full of tortillas and *chiles*, had turned into a sagging, broken-hearted crust.

Of course, no one knew if any of this was true. Just as no one knew if Casper had actually ordered that beer in Trebol's tavern— Trebol always swore to this as fact, but Trebol was also known as the neighborhood's King of Bullshit. In truth, none of it mattered anyway. No one really cared if the stories had been passed down with accuracy or not, because the one thing everyone was sure of was that even though Casper had been a notorious drug addict, one whose drug of choice had been marijuana joints dipped in embalming fluid, it was during one of his highs that he came up with the ridiculous idea to get all the gangs in the neighborhood together. And even though he had been shot the moment he stepped into Latin Counts territory, shot by the first gang he'd tried to approach, in that instant he yelled "Truce," he had made a completely heartfelt attempt at doing something in his life.

BLOOD

Make eye contact with everyone in the bar, everyone that walks in. Sit where you get a good view of the front door. Keep an eye on the bathroom; you never know what's going to come out. Make sure you know where all the exits are. Be careful of a small guy who talks a lot of shit—he can usually back it up. These are the rules, little man, this is how it works.

You put money on the counter only when you're positive you can. No one will talk shit if you don't, but if you do and you don't look like you know what you're doing, you're a mark. Guys that come in here and don't look the bartender in the eye when they order are assholes. You don't need to talk to them. You can't trust a guy who won't look you in the eye. Remember Mustang? Used to live down the block. I don't know if you remember him—you were pretty young then. He knew how to look you in the eye. You can trust a man like that. His old lady shot him. That's the way it goes.

See how I sit here, elbows on the bar sometimes, sometimes

leaning back. That's fine. Never put your head on the bar—you look like a fool. Rule number one: never look like a fool. If you know how to drink you can sit here all day long and never get drunk, just ride the same high, worst you get is a nasty headache—take aspirin for that shit. Dave Belmarez, Chorizo's son, he used to come in here. Big guy, weighed two-fifty easy, six-foot-something, biggest Mexican I ever seen. Couldn't drink for shit. Used to come in here and get fucked up, useless. Threw up on the bar once. Vincie, the bartender, had to put him out on the sidewalk. Needed six guys to help him— ain't that right, Vincie? See, Vincie knows the score. Chorizo can't even come in here no more. He's embarrassed. I would be too. Slow, little man, that's how you take it. You can go all night.

It'll happen to you once. Someone will step up. Someone won't come up behind you and call you out—that shit only happens in the movies. But someone will challenge your ass, guaranteed—be staring at you from across the bar, looking at the back of your head so you can feel it. You just look them straight in the eye. Don't even make a move, just make eye contact. Then you ask "What's up?" Only you do it like you're putting money on the bar, like you know your shit. If you say it right, everything's cool. If they smile and turn away, you know you're cool, but if you fuck it up, and you'll know you did if they just stand there, hard as a rock, you're going to have to go at it. It's all right, Vincie knows you're my brother—but if you back down, that shit's with you forever. People remember that shit.

You see that thing sitting down there, hunched over like he got a lump on his back? Well, he does. That's Sammy. He's a mope, a drunk, been one all his life. Got that lump from leaning over bars. He can tell you about when the neighborhood was all Polish. I bet you didn't even know that. See, you learn shit. Bet you thought it was always Mexican. Hell no, the Polacks were here first. That's what Sammy is—a Polack. Shit, I bet he's the only one left, him and his mother. He lives with her over on Coulter Avenue. You see that stool he's on? Tony from Mitchell's Lumber built it for him. That's Sammy's stool. You don't ever sit on it—you're damn right that's a seat belt. He fell off his stool so many times they put a seat belt on that motherfucker. Doesn't work, though. He just falls over and the stool follows him. It's worse than before.

People fuck with Sammy, but you better not, ever. He won the lottery once, one of those scratch-and-win deals. Won six hundred dollars. Came in here with a woman. Trixie—that's her real name. Sounds phony too, don't it? She lives by the hamburger joint on Eighteenth. When she came in here wrapped around Sammy, the whole bar stood up and clapped. She's a whore but it don't matter, not for Sammy. He bought everyone a round. Bought his lady some fluffy drink, schnapps—never drink schnapps, schnapps is for pussies. Trixie just sat there, looking sophisticated, next to Sammy and his seat-belt chair. She had her legs crossed, all scarred up, bruises, like she been in the alley awhile, but that's all right, Sammy hadn't been with a lady since World War II; he can tell you about that too, World War II. That's why you respect him. He's got history. He knows shit, like an old uncle.

That back door over there leads to the alley. If you have to, your aunt Hildy's house is two blocks down. If the heat's really on, you can climb the porch right in back. That's Chorizo's house. You just tell him you're my brother. Only if someone comes in here shooting shit up, that's where everyone's running. Think about that. Vincie don't let nobody get behind the bar—remember that too. You see a guy come in with a wheelchair, be careful, watch that shit. The trench coats are obvious, people don't do that anymore. They like wheelchairs now—I don't know why. Farmer Dave was telling me about Martin's hot dog stand over on Twenty-Third. Got held up by these two niggers, one was in a wheelchair. Those boys won't be coming back, though. Martin's gunning for them. He used to keep a .38 behind the counter; he's got a shotgun now, short barrel, calls it his ghetto blaster. Farmer Dave got it for him.

One time this boy came in here looking for Indio—you know, one of the Deluna brothers. They were hanging out in here for a while, but they stopped. People were driving by throwing bottles at the front door. It was only a matter of time before they started shooting up the joint. So Vincie tells them, "Why don't you motherfuckers go back to your own corner?" Problem is Eddie Deluna drinks in here. He's the older brother. Don't ever tangle with him. If he ever bothers you, you tell me. He opens his mouth one more time and I'm going to kill his ass. I don't give a shit—jail time is worth that motherfucker. He's a hothead, that's all he is. Has to be a hard-ass because he's a pussy. You see Mario over there fucking with anybody? No, and you never will. He's been in and out of jail more times than anyone can count. Fucking Eddie wishes he was like that.

Anyway, those bullet holes in the bar—move those ashtrays—that's what that boy did who was looking for Indio. He ran out of bullets. Had a little .25, everybody was laughing. First, because this asshole shows up with a cap gun. Second, because he's firing away, screaming and shit, and didn't hit nothing but the bar and a couple of stools. They beat his ass, Vincie and a couple of other guys, even

Sammy. Dumped him out there for the dogs. Vincie called up Eddie. The Deluna brothers beat his ass even more, put him in the hospital.

Most of the guys in here are Disciples. When you get sent to prison, that's who you run with. You know the names. If you get sent to the County, you say my name and Mario's—they'll take care of you. If you get sent downstate, mention your uncle Big Ray—they'll take care of you there. Only never ever mention Eddie Deluna. You're a mark if you do. Eddie got locked up in the County two years ago for beating up some bagger at the A&P. Eddie ran with the Kings in there. He's a phony, don't even mess with that scum.

Cisco too. He's that Puerto Rican who lives on Twenty-First. He never comes in here, though—everyone's got it out for him. He's got no respect. He gets his ass kicked, gets all wickied up, then wants to start shit again. Same people keep beating his ass. That's not respect, that's stupidity. He took a cigarette from Sammy's mouth once, snatched it right out like Sammy was some kind of punk. Sammy can't defend himself, so Vincie beat Cisco's ass. You'll probably have to beat his ass too. If you don't beat his ass, fuck it—you're still young. If it's just Cisco, you can shrug it off, only never step down, nowhere. If he comes up to you, you just stand there, little man. He beats his wife. She's fine too. They got two kids. Once I was out front of Bogart's house, on Twenty-First. Cisco lives right across the street. We're out there having some beers, shooting the shit, and here comes Cisco's lady, running across the street, one shoe on; Cisco following her ass, calling her a puta, a whore, all these other crazy, nasty names. She fell in the middle of the street, tripped over the sewer cover. I remember what she said too. She looks up at Cisco and says, "Cisco, I don't know why you hit me—I love you so much and you keep on hitting me." You know what Cisco did? He kicked her in the face. Kicked her right in the fucking face, broke her nose, blood all over. Fuck that. Me and Bogart broke Cisco's nose. He knows not to pull that shit around us. That's why Eddie Deluna is always talking shit. Those two are best friends, probably been fucking each other since grammar school. That's why you'll have trouble with them. Cisco you can handle, not Eddie. When they start calling your brother a pussy, you beat Cisco's ass, and tell me about Eddie. Next chance I get, I'm going to kill that son of a bitch.

You better never fuck with drugs. You can smoke a little pot—shit's harmless—but you motherfucker better never mess with that hardcore shit. I'll beat your ass if I ever find any on you. You can't think right, then when you need to move fast, figure shit out, you're on low gear, you get swallowed up. That's what happens. That's how it works. The neighborhood wasn't like that before. Not when I was coming up. These boys weren't into drugs. It was all turf. That sounds stupid to you now, but that's because you got these idiots surrounding you. Not before, though. It was all respect.

There was this boy named Jap. I used to run with him when we lived over on May Street. We used to hang over at Dvorak Park, where they had the sprinkler and shit, all the kids running through there. Remember, I used to take you? Anyway, Jap had this fine lady. And I'll tell you, you don't know fine until you seen this girl. You probably think you do, that little chicken girlfriend you got, nipples like raisins, but this girl was fine. She was probably sixteen or so, long hair. She wasn't fucked up, like most of these girls that hang around. No, this girl was from a hardcore family, stone Mexican, traditional. Her name was Elsie or something, maybe Laura, but everyone was after her. So there was this other boy, Junebug, a Latin Count, fat dude, stinky, nobody liked him because he was always starting shit, and Junebug decides to have this party. It's a Saturday night, everyone from the neighborhood's there—everything's cool. Then Junebug starts rapping to Jap's lady, asking her if she wants to have his babies, if she's still a virgin, stupid shit like that. Jap's standing right there, so he steps up to Junebug and warns him. He says to Junebug, "You mess with my lady again and I'll kill you." Damn if that wasn't some badass shit. Said it just like Clint Eastwood too. You mess with my lady again and I'll kill you. See? That's how it was. You could talk shit. You had time to be cool. Well, Junebug didn't care. He figured Jap was just a young stud, full of shit. So Junebug wanders around the party some more, gets a little more juiced up, then rides up behind Jap's lady and just grabs her ass. Mean motherfucker. Reaches around and starts fondling her chest, ripping at her clothes. Next thing you know Jap runs out the door and comes back in about three minutes with his old man's .38. Jacked that motherfucker up. Shot Junebug six times right in the chest. Dead on arrival. No chance. Jap got fifteen years. Served four. He's out in Aurora now, married that girl. Elsie I think her name was, maybe Laura.

That's how it was when I came up. People would give warnings. It was almost fun, like a story. Like if you were to write the damn thing out you would say, 'and the motherfucker said it just like Clint Eastwood.' Now people don't give a shit. You know why all these girls get knocked up? Because at one time it meant something. A few boys would skip out on their old ladies, but most of the time when you had a kid, that was your family. Everybody would talk shit. "Damn, you're with her forever now, bro." And the boy would smile and say all proud, "Yeah, I know." Then we'd talk about it. Ask him, "When's the wedding?" and "Is her old man pissed off?" That's how it was. That's when people were stand-up. Defend what's in their heart, not what they can sell. You got a good friend, that means you do anything for them. That's being stand-up. If he's broke, you give him a handout, you never ask for it back. If he gets into some shit with some boys out front, you step out there and back him up, even when he's the one who's wrong. A friend's all you got, they're family, and once you don't got family, tell me, motherfucker, what do you got?

BLUE MAGIC

THE EDGE

For one summer I lived on the edge of the earth. This was when I was small, like six or seven. I lived with my aunt, across the street from a huge gravel park. Across the park there were houses, and then a water tower, and then who knows what, the edge of the earth—I never went any farther.

There was a river there. I could smell it, especially in the morning, or early in the evening, a strong fishy smell, the way a penny tastes. I stayed indoors during those times. The rest of the time I walked.

The edge of the earth was strange. There were highways up on stilts. There were empty churches. There were foghorns. There was the constant hum of traffic, like a swarm of bees hovering just around the corner. After a while the sound was comforting, and when I finally moved back with my parents, after they got back together, it took weeks before I could actually sleep a night the whole way through.

My aunt used to walk with me. She was young. She was very pretty. When we walked men whistled at her. I shot them dirty looks. They paid me no mind. My aunt didn't seem to care one way or another.

Our trips happened at night, after dinner, after the river smell had passed, or receded back into the river as I imagined it did.

"Where does that smell come from?" I asked her.

"The fish," she said. "Didn't you ever see the fish floating on top?"

"No."

"We should come out in the day sometime. You'll see the dead fish, how they float on the top."

"Do you think the group KISS are really devil worshippers?"

"No, I don't think they worship the devil. But I think maybe they know some kind of magic."

"Do you think they ever take off their makeup?"

"No. They do everything with their makeup on. They even sleep with it on. They never take it off."

My aunt and I had conversations like this as we walked down the broken streets of our neighborhood. We always moved along the same route, starting out toward downtown, the big buildings of the Loop, then turning up and over the railway viaduct, then moving down by the shrimp store, then over the river. We were always on the edge, skirting the lines, the boundaries. I often felt that one step too far to the left would cause the earth to crumble beneath my feet, and off I would tumble into darkness, nothingness, my aunt looking down at me, her hair blowing in the wind, a look on her face like she'd seen things like this happen before.

We stole the ladder from Fat Javy's house. It was in his gangway. He should've had it locked up.

Sergio was more drunk than me. We laughed as we walked down Javy's gangway. I remember Javy opening his window and saying something. I remember Sergio saying something back. I wish I could remember what it was now. It was funny as hell.

We walked down Twenty-First Place. Sergio was in the front. I was in the back. The streets were empty. It was late. We had school the next morning.

I remember now. I remember Little Joseph opened his screen door. It was warm that night, like close to the end of the school year. Little Joseph, who was eight or nine at the time, opened his screen door and asked us: "What are you guys doing?"

"Shhhh," Sergio told him. "We're breaking into Yesenia's house." We started laughing again. Little Joseph looked at me and smiled, then he closed his screen door. When Little Joseph was fourteen he was stabbed to death by his girlfriend, a girl who everyone said "loved him too much." It's funny how you remember things, a word or two, a scene you carry with you for the rest of your life. *What are you guys doing?* I remember Little Joseph.

We got to Yesenia's building. Sergio said he knew where her bedroom was. "Right here," he said. "It's this one. I'm positive."

We placed the ladder up against the wall. She lived on the second floor. The top of the ladder rested just below the window ledge.

"Hold on to it tight," I said to Sergio.

"All right," he said.

I began to climb.

It was a long climb, longer than I'd expected. Halfway up I stopped to rest my arms. I looked up the block. Streetlamp poles sliced long, thin shadows across the orange-tinted sidewalk. An L train rumbled over Hoyne Avenue then disappeared behind the Lutheran church. I looked down to Sergio. His face was bright orange with streetlight.

"Hey, bro," he whispered loudly to me. "Tell her you love her." He started to laugh.

"Fuck you," I said down to him.

And then I turned and continued to climb.

BLUE MAGIC

S he made me dance. It was her. I never wanted to.

She was drunk. I knew she was when she started to smoke the Kools she bummed off my aunt Stephanie, or my father's Winstons when Stephanie had run out. She'd hold the cigarette between two fingers and with her remaining fingers hold on to my small hand. In those days I was just barely tall enough to stare at her breasts, but I didn't. I looked down at our feet, my dirty white socks, her bare, dark toes. She was a natural barefooter. It was in her blood.

"No, no," she corrected. "Like this, *Mm, mm—mm, mm.*" She moved to the Chi-Lites, the Delfonics. She swung her hips, stepped in a way that appeared entirely light. I followed her movements. "Listen to the song," she corrected. "There... there you go... right... that's it." At this point I closed my eyes.

I don't remember much after that, at our parties. The feeling

I remember after closing my eyes is something similar to what I felt as a drunk teenager, cruising with my partners, time and distance nonexistent.

For me, our parties always ended up this way. I remember small things, people laughing, cursing. I remember my aunt Chefa cackling, that laugh she used to have. I remember my cousin Bobby fistfighting with my aunt Bernice's boyfriend, Fabian. I remember bottles of wine, clinks of glasses. I remember the Stylistics, Blue Magic. I remember death being something that happened to people I didn't even know, ancient, gray people from Mexico or Poland, places I'd never seen, places I could only imagine. And I remember a song called "I Do Love You." And if I could, I would take my mother in my arms again, and I would dance with her to that song, which went, "*I do love you, Ooo-oo-o, yes I do, girl.*"

GROWING PAINS

They sat at the edge of the sprinkler pool, the two of them, a boy who spoke no Spanish and his grandmother just in from Mexico. He reached for his shoes, Daniel. He reached down to take off his shoes and immediately his grandmother moved to help. She untied the left, then the right, then paired them up and placed them between her and her grandson. She patted them as if they were alive.

She wasn't much taller than him. As they sat there together it seemed in fact that Daniel was taller than his grandmother. But she was wide. Not fat or even heavyset, just wide, like a tank or a bulldozer is wide. Daniel looked at her arm. She wore a dark flannel long-sleeve shirt. She'd worn long-sleeves for the past week, ever since she'd arrived in the States. It was mid-August in Chicago, hot, humid. Still, Daniel thought, she was from Mexico. Chicago summers were just too cold for her.

He looked up and noticed his grandmother was staring at his

feet. He was wearing dirty socks. Daniel had known that they would end up at the sprinkler pool today. He had known his grandmother would ask him if he wanted to go in: she'd done the same thing every day since she'd arrived. But he'd put on dirty socks anyway. There were cleaner ones in the dirty pile, Daniel knew. But he'd simply grabbed the first pair he found, a pair lying on the floor next to the dirty basket. Now he hesitated before reaching to pull them off.

His grandmother sighed. She looked up across the park, focusing her beady eyes on something far away. She looked back to him. "*Pues*," she said. "*Andale*." She clapped her hands. "*Andale, andale*." She reached down, grabbed the toe of his left sock and yanked it off. Then she went for the right. She held the socks up in front of her. For a moment Daniel thought she might bring them to her nose for a smell. But she only sighed again, then flapped them out. She folded the socks neatly, dirtiest sides in, then tucked them into his shoes. She looked back to him. "*Pues, que tienes?*" she asked. Her voice was squeaky, witchy, like there was a cackle in there somewhere, waiting to come out.

"*Nada*," Daniel answered. But the word came out wrong, the *d* sharp and heavy, the way the word sounded in English. He got to his feet and walked slowly toward the sprinkler. Na-*tha* he told himself. Na-*tha*.

The trip to pick up his grandmother had been only slightly eventful. It could've been worse. He and his mother had made the long trip to the airport in their silver 1978 Ford Granada, the one with the thermostat problem. Daniel didn't understand what the thermostat was and he doubted that his mother did, yet every time the car started smoking and wheezing and eventually stalled, his mother mumbled "Fucking thermostat" as if she knew exactly why it had stopped the car from moving.

His grandmother's flight was to arrive at 1:25 a.m. That night the air was cool and damp, the type of heavy night that forecasted the end of summer, the coming school year. It was the type of weather that gave Daniel his aches, or *rumas*, as his mother called them: the "Mexican pains."

"Good thing it's cool out tonight," his mother said as they pulled onto the expressway. "Fucking thermostat might actually work." Daniel moaned. Above them long rows of streetlamps stretched off into the distance. Shadows from each light pole flickered through the car's interior, strobing what little light there was. Down below, to either side of the expressway, the lamps at street level held wide orange halos of humidity.

They approached Eighteenth Street, Providence of God Church. Just around the corner lived his great-uncle Max, whom he hadn't seen in two years, who'd raised his mother when she first moved to Chicago. When Daniel was younger, his cousins, Max's daughters, had babysat him. They were more like aunts back then, more like sisters to his mother, the way she had lived with them. They used to take him on long walks around the neighborhood and he remembered how the expressway sounded from underneath, the high whine of tires, the low drone of truck engines, the shudder of engine brakes. Where he and his mother lived now, Twenty-Second Street, was in the same neighborhood, just farther away from the expressway. Still, on clear nights the sound of travel could be heard through Daniel's window and it helped him get to sleep.

They passed the Sears Tower, the city skyline. He looked out to the Morton Salt factory, its blue corrugated roof lit up bright, M-O-R-T-O-N spelled out in large white block letters. A wave of pain shot through his knees. He flinched.

"What, you got your *rumas* again?" his mother asked. At the steering wheel, between two fingers, his mother held a Newport 100. The embers glowed a bright red, pulsing with the air rushing in through her open window.

"Maybe it's time to take you back to the doctor," she said.

"I don't need to go the doctor," Daniel replied. "It'll go away." He reached down and began massaging his knees.

"It's up to you," his mother said. "I'd go, though." She brought the cigarette to her mouth.

When Daniel was a young boy his mother had taken him to four separate doctors, pediatricians. Finally she had taken him to a fifth, a geriatrician, looking for some answers about the arthritic-like pains Daniel was experiencing in his joints. "Just growing pains," they all said. "He'll outgrow them." They all said this with a smile. They all patted him on the head and called him "Sport."

Daniel had yet to outgrow his growing pains. He was now ten years old. Whenever the weather changed, whenever the air was thick and wet, Daniel felt his joints swell and stiffen. When he was younger the ache had been so bad he'd had to soak in steaming hot baths for hours at a time. He often wasn't able to sleep and instead would sit and cry until his mother came into his room with the Ben-gay. Now, at his older age, Daniel had come to accept the pains like one does an annoying relative: just put up with them, they'll eventually go away. In his sock drawer he kept his own tubes of Ben-gay, two of them, just in case one ran out.

Cool air from his mother's open window swirled around Daniel and his pains. The car had no radio and instead his mother sang Smokey Robinson tunes one after another—"Baby That's Backatcha," "The Love I Saw in You Was Just a Mirage." She hummed the words, stopping only for a Newport inhale, or when she suddenly seemed deep in thought.

"Mom, can't you close your window?" Daniel asked. His mother was quiet for the moment, driving, looking straight ahead. Daniel could see the distance his mother's gaze often assumed, like on days off when she parked herself in front of the TV and watched *The Price Is Right*, or Friday nights, when she watched *Dallas*. Daniel hated that look of his mother's. He thought she looked dumb at those times, helpless.

"Mom," he said again.

"What, baby?" his mother asked. She reached across her body and tapped her cigarette on the top edge of her window.

"Your window," Daniel said. "Can't you close it?"

"Oh. Sorry," she said. She took one last inhale, then made a motion to throw the cigarette out. Just before releasing it she stopped and brought it back for a quick, final tug. Then she tossed the butt out the window. In the light of the expressway, Daniel caught sight of the faded green tattoo on the web of his mother's right hand. It was small, a six-pointed star with a *T* in the center. The tattoo had been there since before Daniel was born; he'd grown up with it, but it never failed to catch his eye. When he'd asked about it in the past, the only answer he'd gotten was that it was a club his mother used to belong to. "We did stupid things," his mother said. Daniel knew the truth, that his mother had actually been in a street gang. The Tokers didn't even exist anymore as far as Daniel knew. But some of their graffiti, old and faded, was still scrawled on the factories and warehouses back in their neighborhood.

The fact that his mother's gang no longer existed made Daniel wonder how old his mother really was. She was twenty-eight, Daniel knew. But age wasn't what he thought about when he considered her "being old." Instead Daniel felt like his mother had been someone else entirely before he was born. Someone he wished he knew more about.

His mother exhaled as she rolled up her window. Daniel coughed and waved a hand in front of his face. His mother stared at the road and began humming.

The pains continued. Gradually, with his massaging, the ache transferred from his knees to his hands, and he began kneading his palms. This was how the process usually went. On a bad night he'd go through a massage of nearly every joint in his body, the pain switching locations constantly, as if his rubbing actually chased it to the next set of joints. Alongside him his mother fell silent again. Daniel began concentrating on the car, listening for the pangs that announced the engine was about to smoke and stall.

He was happy to be going to the airport. The last time he'd been there was two years earlier, when he and his mother had gone to pick up Birdy, his mother's childhood friend. Birdy and his mother had grown up as neighbors. Birdy had worked for Bell Telephone and been transferred to Sacramento, California. *Sacramento*. The word had always sounded warm and tropical to Daniel. His mother had had the opportunity to go. At least according to Birdy. "Sunny California," Birdy said that first night of her visit. "You guys could be living there right this very second, blue skies, valley air." Daniel was sitting across from Birdy. He had been listening to her tell stories about his mother's past. "Could've taken you, Maggie." That's what Birdy called his mother, that's what most people called her, friends she would see on the street, friends from a long time ago. Magdalena was her real name. "Could be working right next to me," Birdy continued. "Partying like the old days. But nope, never, can't do the easy thing, right?" Birdy reached for her rum and Coke. At the table his mother rattled the ice in her glass. "I offered," Birdy said to Daniel. She leaned over the table and whispered, "I think there was a man involved." Birdy's breath was sharp with liquor. Daniel smiled. He knew she was talking about his father. Birdy leaned back again. Daniel wanted to hear more. "But hey," Birdy continued. "Don't want no help, don't get no help, right, Maggie?" Birdy sighed and shook her head. She took a sip of her dark drink.

"I'm doing fine right here," Daniel's mother said. She wasn't mad, Daniel could tell from her voice, but he could tell also that she was about to get mad, like this was a warning shot, the kind she gave him about dirty socks, a messy bedroom. *"Clean that room or your ass is grass,"* she often said.

"Uh, yeah, right," Birdy responded. "I like working for asshole lawyers too, my favorite. File this, copy this, get me coffee. Fuck *that*," she said. She looked to Daniel as if giving him the opportunity to add to the list. *Yeah, Mom and I love our house too, I mean apartment. Especially how the toilet leaks, those roaches, great.* Daniel didn't say a word. Birdy took another sip of her drink. Daniel felt his mother's temper then. He felt it take shape in the blank space, after Birdy's last word.

"You think I need to hear from you how my life is going?" Daniel's mother asked. Her voice started to rise. "I got enough people think they know what's good for me." Daniel wondered who his mother could be talking about. "Fuck California," his mother said sharply. "You think I give a shit about California…" Daniel rolled his eyes.

"Maggie, calm down. I was just saying. Relax," Birdy said.

"Who do I need to relax for?" his mother asked. "You? You come into my house and tell me how to live. Fuck you. Fuck California."

Daniel put his chin down on his arms.

"Maggie, *calmate*. I was just talking, girl. It's my opinion. Don't do anything, do whatever you want. I don't care."

"I know I can do what I want. I don't need you to tell me what I can do. Fuck all of you think I need guidance." Daniel watched as his mother fumed. Her forehead was wrinkled. She looked ready to smack somebody's head off.

After a moment Birdy leaned into Daniel. "You know, she used to be worse," Birdy said. "You think she's bad now." She raised her eyebrows.

There was a long silence. Eventually Daniel got up and went to his bedroom. Later that night he awoke to music. "The Agony and the Ecstasy." He could hear his mother singing. Birdy too. He knew his mother was happy. He fell back to sleep.

*   *   *

His mother turned off the expressway. A few more minutes and they were at the airport entrance. A sign over the right-hand lane said what seemed like fifty different things:

BAGGAGE PICK-UP

UNITED PARCEL SERVICE

TERMINALS 1, 2, 3, 4

INTERNATIONAL TERMINALS 1, 2, 3, 4

CAR RENTAL

    HERTZ

    INTERNATIONAL

Beneath each number, in even smaller print, was a list of the airlines each terminal serviced. Over the left lane another sign read: PARKING, OVERNIGHT PARKING... Daniel couldn't read the rest. His mother pulled into the left lane and followed it around a curve.

"Did you see *Mex-a-cana* up there?" his mother asked.

"No," Daniel replied.

His mother started to ask another question, started to say something, but Daniel caught sight of a large, bright billboard and stopped paying attention. AIR JAMAICA, the sign read. In the background were palm trees, sky-blue water, a pink flamingo. Daniel thought the billboard was so huge passengers taking off could read it. Then Daniel saw another billboard, this one to the left, across the road. UNITED AIRLINES. In the corner a British flag blew in a breeze. Big Ben stood in the background, bold and bright—Daniel had read about Big Ben once in school. He turned his head to follow the sign. As his mother drove past, the sign's backside showed up pitch-black like a lost opportunity. He wondered if people came to the airport with nowhere to go. He wondered if there were some people so rich they could just look at a billboard and say, "Ah, England, that's where I'll go, see Big Ben."

"Mom," he said. "Would you ever go to England?"

"Sure," she said. "You going to take me?"

"Yes," Daniel said.

"Fine," she answered. "I'll pack when we get home." She turned into the parking garage. "We'll leave your grandma here."

They found an empty spot after three floors of searching. Daniel stepped out of the car. Immediately he recognized the smell of airplane exhaust. He took a deep breath. Back home the slightest whiff of truck or car exhaust started him retching, prompted an instantaneous headache. But here, airplane exhaust, he didn't mind. It meant travel, long-distance travel. And there was noise. Even at this hour, 1:15 a.m., people were walking. There was luggage. There was traffic. Not delivery vans grinding through gears, not sixteen ice cream trucks playing "Pop Goes the Weasel" over and over, but a different kind of traffic, a quiet traffic, things moving, flowing, like air pressure releasing when a bus comes to a stop.

The terminal's automatic doors slid open. Daniel's mother walked fast. She was oblivious. Daniel, on the other hand, walked slow, pimped even, strutted, like the gangbangers did out in front of his apartment building. At one point his mother stopped and held out her hand for him. She snapped twice rapidly, her bright red fingernails reflecting the sharp, fluorescent light of the airport. Daniel caught sight of his mother's tattoo. He took her hand and followed her for a quick few steps. Then he let go and began strutting again.

His mother walked to one of the monitors hanging high in metal cabinets behind the benches.

"Mex-a-cana. Mex-a-cana."

She was saying it wrong. Daniel knew. Me-*he*-cana, it should've been pronounced. Daniel repeated the word to himself.

"Mom, how come we don't speak Spanish at home?"

His mother sighed. "I don't know, Daniel. We're late. If your grandmother has to wait five fucking minutes I'll hear about it for the next two months."

They walked quickly through the terminal. His mother's short heels snapped hard against the tiled floor.

In the week before his grandmother's arrival, Daniel had heard more about his grandmother than ever before. In the past she had always been an unmentioned subject. He knew he had a grandmother; he'd seen pictures. But she was never talked about. The few times his grandmother had ever called, long-distance, Daniel hadn't known until after his mother had hung up. "That was your grandmother," his mother would say, exasperated. Then she would take a seat on the couch and stare at the television set, that distant look on her face, never a word about the actual conversation.

But in the last week there'd been a grandmother story for every day. "She'll say anything to get what she wants," one story went. "She won't even say she's hungry. Instead she says, *You look hungry.* What is that? Don't trust her. I don't. Why do you think I left?" Daniel had heard that one before. How his mother, when she was eleven, had left Mexico to come live with her uncle in Chicago. He had heard the story from his cousins. How his mother had left his "crazy" grandmother. How his mother had taken a bus alone all the way from Monterrey, Mexico. During that conversation his cousins had made small, biting comments—"*Why do you think his mother's so crazy?*" "*Like mother like daughter.*" When Daniel asked his mother about what his cousins had said, his mother replied, "Yeah, well, your cousins are nuts too. Don't forget I left them also."

Daniel had heard this story before as well. How his mother's pregnancy had angered her great-uncle. How the family had stopped talking to her. Soon after Daniel brought up what his cousins had said, his mother stopped dropping him off there for babysitting.

That was two years ago. They'd seen his cousins again recently, stepping out of Providence of God Church while he and his mother were driving to the laundromat. "Duck," his mother said. "Your cousins." And he and his mother sped by completely unnoticed.

Where they had gone before, when Birdy had arrived, was upstairs. Mexicana Airlines flights seemed to arrive in the airport's basement. There were no windows in the terminal, just rows of orange padded seats, and more people, it seemed to Daniel, than he had seen in the entire airport. The room smelled of perfume and it all reminded Daniel of the supermarkets back in his neighborhood, the crying babies, the cowboy hats.

"*Vuelo diez-cuarenta,*" his mother said to the attendant behind the counter. Daniel was startled. He was always startled when he heard his mother speak Spanish. He knew she could speak the language, but she did it so rarely that whenever Daniel heard her, how crisp and sharp she could sound, he was surprised.

The attendant said something back. She said it so fast Daniel couldn't understand.

"Whew, not here yet," his mother said.

Daniel's mother turned. He followed, listening to her heels, watching her part the sea of people the way she'd always been able to do.

She stopped at the end of a row of seats. All were taken.

"*Por favor*," a man in a cowboy hat said. He rose from his chair at the end of the row. "Please, sit down here."

"*Gracias*," Daniel's mother said. She walked to the chair and ushered Daniel into it. She put her purse down in his lap. The man remained standing next to Daniel's mother. Daniel waited for the man to start speaking. In the clinics at home this always happened. Men offered his mother seats and they wanted conversation in return. Daniel knew they probably wanted more, a phone number, a date. His mother flipped her dark hair over her shoulder in the direction of the man next to her.

There was definitely something confusing about Mexicana. Every few minutes the attendant behind the counter made an announcement and each time some of the crowd moved to the left, and a new group filled in the open spaces. Along a glass wall people were standing, duffel bags hanging from their shoulders. Suitcases lay on their sides on the floor, and on some of these children sat.

Another announcement and Daniel's mother reached out her hand. Daniel got to his feet. The man stepped aside and watched them leave. They walked down a long corridor. Before turning into a separate room, Daniel took one last look behind him. The man was still staring. Daniel almost raised a hand to say goodbye.

The room was already packed. Daniel's mother got up on her toes and looked around. "There she is," his mother said. She led him though another maze of people. Daniel had never seen his grandmother in person. In her pictures she had looked nice enough, normal. Still, after all he'd heard, he'd expected to see an ugly, gnarled brute of woman. He was surprised when he finally saw her.

More than anything, she was short. She had her head away from him but Daniel recognized her, her glasses, how the stems connected high up on her frames then dipped to become the earpieces. Of all the things Daniel had heard, nothing really prepared him for how tiny she was. She was barely taller than him, like it could've been her shoes giving her a boost. His mother said fifteen children had come from this woman. Daniel wondered how that was possible.

Her arms were long. She looked strong, compact, wide. The closer Daniel got, the more he figured she could knock down a tree if she wanted. She looked nothing like his mother. His mother had soft features—her eyebrows, her nose all seemed to mold into each other, but his grandmother was chiseled, sharp and defined. The lines in her face were deep and more like scars than wrinkles.

"*Hola, mamá,*" his mother said. "*Comó estas?*"

His grandmother jumped. "*Ay, mija, me asustastes. Comó estas mi vida?*"

His mother leaned in and gave his grandmother a kiss. His grandmother returned the kiss, then said something Daniel couldn't understand. He saw an angry look on his mother's face.

"*Y tú?*" his grandmother said to him. "*Éres Daniel, verdad?*"

"*Sí,*" Daniel said. And she gave him a kiss and hugged him. He still couldn't believe how short she was. Daniel tried to hug her back but he felt like he couldn't get a grip. He felt like he was hugging a building. When his grandmother backed away, he wasn't satisfied.

She rubbed the back of his head. "*Tan flaquillo, te pareces a tú abuelito.*"

"*Mí papá no era flaco, mamá,*" his mother said.

"*Enflacó antes de morir. Pero tú ya no estavas.*"

Daniel had no idea what his mother and grandmother were saying to each other, but he could tell there was an edge to it. His mother shook her head and without a word picked up his grandmother's suitcase and began walking away. His grandmother looked to Daniel as if she had something to say, but all she did was pull him close. Together they walked in his mother's wake.

This had all happened one week ago. Since that time they had visited his great-uncle exactly once. There had been more tension in the air than ever before. Hardly anything had been said during the visit. Voices were hushed. Daniel was the main topic of conversation. "Is he doing good in school?" "Summer break, huh?" "Make sure he drinks a lot, dehydration, you know?"

During the visit his great-uncle said a total of two words to his sister, Daniel's grandmother: "Hi" and "Bye."

Daniel, his grandmother, and his mother left after only an hour. When they got back to the car his grandmother and mother went back and forth like schoolgirls. Daniel couldn't understand everything they were saying, but he knew they were talking about his great-uncle and cousins, and not in a positive way. His grandmother and mother laughed and waved their hands. Then they said things and laughed and waved their hands again. It was the only time all week that they seemed at all alike. It was the only time all week that they seemed the least bit happy with each other.

Between Daniel and his grandmother, though, things were different. There had been cold nights, damp nights, like the night of his grandmother's arrival. Daniel had experienced his *rumas* often, and while his mother had taken to leaving him to his own remedies, his grandmother went out of her way to make him more comfortable. She drew baths for him, something his mother hadn't done for him in years. His grandmother had also cut tube socks for him, taking the toes off of an old pair so that he could use them as warmers once he put his Ben-gay on. When he went to bed now, with his *rumas*, tube socks around his elbows and knees, he was in a world of warmth, heaven.

Daniel had also improved his Spanish. In the last week he had learned the right way to roll his *r*'s. His grandmother spoke to him in Spanish, so he had to understand, and more than that, he had to respond. If he was unsure of a word, he used those he knew and got as close as possible. Then his grandmother would say, "Ahh, *cacahuete*," or whatever she guessed the word was. Somehow, Daniel knew instantly if the word his grandmother quoted was the word he meant. If it was, Daniel would nod, say it over to himself, and commit it to memory.

Between his mother and grandmother, things were more tense. Aside from that brief moment after visiting his great-uncle, the two of them argued constantly. Sometimes his grandmother tired of arguing and dealt quietly with whatever his mother said. Sometimes it was the other way around, and his mother put up with whatever his grandmother said. But most often neither could stand the other, and they would walk around the kitchen cooking or cleaning and at the same time arguing, his grandmother's voice screeching, his mother's voice sounding amazingly similar. When they got to fighting like that, even sitting in his room with the door closed didn't help, and Daniel would leave the apartment to walk the neighborhood, where it was quieter, where at least he was able to think.

Daniel wondered if he'd eventually get to be the same way. If he'd get to the point where being in the same room with his mother was almost physically painful. Already he felt himself wanting to say things—"Mom, can't you just shut up for a minute? What the hell is your problem?" It wasn't so much that he suddenly loved his grandmother and would take her side over anyone else's, it was just that he wanted things to go more smoothly, more smoothly than it seemed they ever could.

At the sprinkler pool Daniel could've made things easier by wearing clean socks. His mother would've said something if she'd seen the ones Daniel had on. Especially considering that there were probably clean ones in his dresser drawer. As it was, he knew that as soon as he and his grandmother returned home from the park, she would take the socks she had pulled off his feet and scrub them the way she did all the white clothes, in the kitchen sink, on the washboard she'd insisted on buying the first day she was in Chicago. She would use gallons of bleach, Daniel knew. She had used so much already that the apartment had begun to smell sour. A smell Daniel was convinced had fumigated all the cockroaches in their apartment building.

As he got up and walked through the wading pool to the sprinkler, Daniel thought about what it must be like in Mexico: if his grandmother had separated herself from her whole family the way his mother had separated herself from everyone here. He wondered about his uncles, his aunts. Fourteen of them. He wondered at the cousins he had running around. He wanted to meet them, visit them, stay with them. He wondered if his grandmother even talked to them, or if all her children, like his mother, had cut her off.

He soaked himself in the cool shower of water. He felt a cold tingle between his legs as the water flooded his jean shorts. He ran his fingers through his hair. He saw the kids around him, some older, dancing and running, some babies, wading near his grandmother. Through the rain of the sprinkler he looked to his grandmother. She had rolled up her long flannel sleeves, and for the first time Daniel saw her forearms. She had tattoos, two or three of them on each arm. They were dull green, the same color as the rusting chain-link fence that surrounded the wading pool. Even from this distance he could see how the ink had bled into her dark skin, how time had created large splotches on her arms rather than anything even or clear. His grandmother was looking off to the left. He knew she would roll down her sleeves as soon as he returned. He wondered how much else he didn't know about his family, how at ten years old he was completely unsure of who he was.

SACRIFICE

Our oldest just turned five. I've always been honest with him. And now I wonder if I should tell him I killed his father.

He is her child; I adopted him. I told Blanca I wanted to. I am not so sure she cared. My wife is a pretty woman, striking even. But she is also desperate. Desperate in the sense that she knows to take what she can get. Desperate in the sense that she knows not to ask for more. I've always given her the most I could. For this reason we don't argue much.

I love her. Don't get me wrong. Although after all these years, after two children, I am not entirely convinced she loves me. But this is not important. Because, you see, I am a desperate man, and my only wish is to come home to a family. Children who call me Daddy and a wife who will never cheat. In many ways our marriage seems born of convenience. Such is the case with desperate people.

Her boy, our boy, turned five in December. His name is Prince

Marcus; I don't like the name. He was named after his father, and so the boy is cursed. Each time I speak or hear our son's name, I am reminded of the man I killed four months ago in the alley three blocks down from where we live. I walk by there often. I need to in order to get to the supermarket. And I look down the alley and expect to see his body there, slumped over, perfectly camouflaged like a bag of trash next to an overflowing garbage can.

I didn't know him personally, not before I married Blanca. He was from Eighteenth Street, and in this neighborhood Eighteenth Street and Twenty-Second Street are night and day, two opposite sides of the universe. He really should've known better than to come around. I suppose the fact that he didn't respect the obvious made me dislike him even more.

Marcus was the leader of the Laflin Lovers. His name on the street was *Prince* Marcus. The Laflin Lovers were not a big gang. They were one of hundreds in our neighborhood, thirty or so members, two or three street corners' worth of turf. But the Laflin Lovers had a reputation. They were crazy. They jumped rivals in front of families. They pulled drive-bys in front of schools, churches. I'd heard of Prince Marcus long before I ever met Blanca. And then there was Orejas, Pac-Man, Lepke—all Laflin Lovers, all with ugly reputations, all under the leadership of Prince Marcus. Maybe this is what attracted my wife.

My wife and Prince Marcus had the fortune of ending up at the exact same school at the exact same time, and when I think about it, timing seems to be the culprit for everything. Benito Juarez High School was built on Blue Island Avenue and Twenty-Second Street, strategically placed to take in kids from both sides of the neighborhood, Twenty-Second *and* Eighteenth. While this was probably the brainstorm of a lifetime for some city planner, it was an unfortunate reality for any kid who couldn't afford an alternative. For the first five years Benito Juarez was up and running, the school had the distinct honor of being the only high school in Chicago with a double-digit murder rate: Cullerton Boys, Two-Ones, Satan Disciples, Latin Brothers, Laflin Lovers, Latin Counts, Latin Bishops, Racine-Boys, Almighty Ambrose all claimed victims. Even in the envelope of my all-boys Catholic high school, I could see that Benito Juarez was the pits. And living in the community that Juarez served, I heard the stories. How Beany from the Two-Ones had stabbed Lil' Cano, from the Party People, in the cafeteria. How Sleepy, who was just a junior Latin Count, was found shot in a stall in the men's room. How Ms. Welzien, one of the PE teachers, had had her nose broken by an Ambrose named Juice. The gangs had taken over. They divided themselves into two categories: Folks and People. Drive-bys began with riders screaming their affiliations—"People!" or "What up, Folks!" Then the shooting started.

There were Chicago police units assigned to Juarez. Their primary job was to pick up the pieces. The wars went on.

It still offends me somewhat that my wife has a history with another man. I know this is petty. Plenty of marriages are actually second and third marriages. But I think my attitude would be different if my wife had been in a relationship with a different kind of guy. The first two years I was with her, I actually got to know Marcus quite well: there was the time he kicked down our front door, the time he threw a brick through the front window of my car while I was driving, the time he nearly OD'd in front of our apartment, puke streaming down his chin onto his black T-shirt. That morning my wife took him in and put him under a cold shower. She knew exactly what to do. She massaged his chest. She gave him blankets, our blankets, and made him chicken noodle soup. He ate breakfast with us, and lunch and dinner, and then the next morning ate another breakfast. At one point he apologized for all he'd ever done. "I'm sorry, Jesse," he told me over scrambled eggs. "I respect you, bro. You know how to keep a woman. You know how to have a family." He cried. My wife put her arm around him. She told him everything was okay. "People in this house love you," she said. I looked at little Prince Marcus, who was too young to love anything at that point, and I wondered who she meant. That afternoon Marcus left. Within a week he had broken into our apartment, through the back door while we were away at work. He didn't take anything. It didn't even appear that he'd gone through any drawers. But he left a note on the kitchen table. *I still luv you, Blanca*, the note said. *I can't help it.* And while it wasn't signed, it was obvious who it was from. My wife cried.

But it's not like I grew up in Winnetka or Arlington Heights or Highland Park. It's not like I took all this lying down. I grew up on Twenty-Second and Oakley. I knew protocol. When he broke in I chased him out of the apartment with a baseball bat. When he used to call late at night and not say anything, I would scream "I'm going to kill you, motherfucker!" into the phone. And then once, after slamming down the phone, I actually went out to hunt for him. I called my partner from when we were young, Ricardo. Ricardo was a Disciple. He'd dropped out of Benito Juarez when it was suspected he'd murdered a Latin Count named Buff. I told Ricardo, "Prince

Marcus is fucking with my family." Within ten minutes Ricardo was outside my door with a .38 automatic, fully loaded. Ricardo knew Prince Marcus. They had gone to Juarez together and had their own history. As I started for the front door, Blanca took a breath to speak. I turned to look and she was holding the phone to her ear, the same phone I had just hung up. With her other arm she was holding little Prince Marcus, using her hip as a ledge for him to sit on. She seemed amazingly young at that moment, small, and for a second I was lost, lost in my own home, married to a woman who had tattoos, a woman who could balance a child on her hip like he was glued there. I didn't know who she had dialed. I wasn't interested in asking. I turned and left the apartment.

"It's chambered," Ricardo said as he handed me the gun. "Careful." The gun was small, nickel-plated. It fit perfectly into my hand. It was the same piece we had used over New Year's to shoot off rounds in Ricardo's gangway. I remembered how quiet it had been. How I'd expected some loud blast but had gotten only a shallow pop that between buildings echoed with a sharp hum.

We cruised Eighteenth Street. We started at Damen Avenue and worked our way east. We slowed down at the taverns, watched who was going in, who was coming out. I held the gun hidden at my thigh, ready to raise it the second I recognized him. At Cirito's pool hall on Blue Island Avenue we pulled to the curb and peered in through the torn black tint that covered the plate-glass windows. On the sidewalk a young girl, a teenager, walked out of a grocery store. She looked into the car as she passed. She saw Ricardo and me and for a quick moment she searched our faces, trying to figure out what we were doing. Something registered. Suddenly the girl turned her head and began walking faster. I looked to Ricardo. He was still studying the pool hall; he hadn't noticed her. I waited for the girl to turn and look again but she never did.

Marcus wasn't there, just a bunch of kids, gangbangers in training, shaved heads, Dago-T's. We pulled away and reached Halsted Street. Then we turned back west. Sweat coated the grip of the gun. I felt as if I was fisting a dirty quarter. I switched hands, flexed my fingers, then wiped my palm on the knee of my jeans. By the time we got to Damen Avenue the gun was under my seat, tucked away in case we got pulled over.

"Want me to turn around?" Ricardo asked.

"No," I said. "He's gone, man. We're not going to find him."

"He's probably fucked up somewhere," Ricardo said. "Angel dust, those Laflin Lovers do angel dust. We should go search some alleys."

I shrugged my shoulders.

Ricardo drove me home.

"It's under the seat," I told him as I climbed out of the car.

"Bro," Ricardo said. "If he comes back just call me. I'll pop him if you don't want to." Then he reached over and pulled the passenger door shut. It was late by then. Or maybe it just seemed late. The streetlights were on. My shadow was pitch-black against the orange-tinted sidewalk. I stuck my key into the door and quietly stepped inside.

But none of this explains who I am. And truth is I am no one. I work at a law firm. I'm a clerk. I make thirty-two thousand dollars a year. I have health insurance and a brand-new Honda. I get on the L at

7:15 a.m. and start work by 8. In the morning I file cases in Circuit Court. Then I eat lunch. Then I file cases in District Court. At some point I am going to finish school. I've been given a promise by my law firm that they will pay my tuition. I am a normal man. I don't wear gold. I don't get high. Things will change. I know they will. I've told my wife this, at night in bed, my arm around her waist. "We'll get a house soon," I've said. "You'll see. Prince will be in a decent school, not that fucking Pickard, where all the gangbanger kids go." My wife never seems to hear. She always has her head turned. I listen for her breathing. I wonder if she is already asleep.

I met my wife in a club called Vincie's on Fifty-Ninth and California. Other than beer advertisements, the only real light in that place was a huge neon sign behind the bar, VINCIE's, in hot-pink illuminated script. I would never have considered Blanca my type, but darkness changes a lot of things and alcohol changes even more. She was pretty, of course, stunning in a familiar kind of way, like you knew who she was, what street she was from, just by looking at her. I'd seen girls like this all my life. Girls that put up a front, a facade you had to scratch through to get to something real. She was sitting at the bar with two other women, and their ugliness seemed to make her stand out. I'd seen them before, all three of them. They were older, more experienced women, like they might really be there just for the drinks. That night I was with Gilbert and Diego, two friends I'd grown up with. I don't know who had had more to drink, my future wife or myself. I don't remember being that drunk, although she says that I was "wasted." She was drunk enough. When Gilbert asked her friend to dance, the girl said she'd go only if Blanca went also. My wife claims to remember that night clearly. How I stumbled when I led her out onto the dance floor. How I couldn't keep the beat and kept holding my hands in the air like a flamenco dancer looking for style points. She still makes fun of me, when she's in a good mood, after the kids are asleep. She giggles and whispers "*Olé*" in my ear. I remember things differently. I remember my wife telling me, "I'm only here to have fun. Don't think this is love." And saying things like this so often it became silly, and we started laughing and telling each other we were "over before we started" and "you can keep the house" and "those kids are mine as much as they are yours." All this while we moved on the dance floor. My wife is a beautiful drunk. Things make more sense to her then. Like at that party for her sister Junie's eighteenth birthday. My wife sat next to me and had me taste her aunt Hilda's *mole*. She kissed me and held her face next to mine for a long time. Then she asked me why I married her.

I told her I'd done it because she was "nothing special" and she seemed to understand what I meant even when I didn't.

Or that time there was a party for her brother Robert when he finished army boot camp. That night she sat on my lap and put her arms around my neck. She fell asleep with her head on my shoulder and I had to carry her to the car while Robert carried Prince. "Later," Robert said to me. "As long as you're good to my sister."

"I am," I said.

He shook my hand and walked away. That was a year after we got married.

It's when my wife is sober that things are slightly more difficult. Maybe reality hits then. Her job with the state—she hates answering phones. The homemade tattoo she has on her right hand, M4E—Marcus For Ever. I've told her we could get rid of it, and we've even gone so far as to ask the gynecologist—because that's where we were when we thought of it. But with everything else going on, my wife's tattoo doesn't seem quite so important. Unless of course it's late at night, and I am reading, and I see her asleep there on the couch, her hand draped across her belly. Marcus For Ever. My wife isn't one to think of the future. I have come to accept that. She was born with nothing and it's a struggle for her to think things could be any different. I don't hold that against her.

Prince Marcus, though, he's a wonderful boy. He's five years old now and he acts like it. He likes to say "shit" and knows it's wrong so he follows every "shit" with an immediate "sorry," as if that makes everything better. After baths he likes to sing and dance naked in front of the mirror, and if he notices us laughing he'll do something even more silly, like act like a monkey or put underwear on his head. With my son I find myself saying over and over, "What is that kid doing?" He looks like his father. He has crazy, thick black hair, the kind that stays up no matter what you put in it. He has sleepy eyes, downturned at the sides as if he's always sad. My wife has since given birth to our daughter, Marisa, and Marisa is the complete opposite of Prince. She's quiet, for one, and calm. She looks like me. She doesn't cry or ask for attention. She just lies in her crib and watches Prince play monkey bars on the furniture. Some nights I bring home McDonald's and Prince goes crazy—he loves Happy Meals. Some nights I bring home Los Comales tacos and my wife goes crazy—she loves their *al pastor*. Some nights I bring home toys for Marisa, stuffed animals, baby puzzles with big pieces that are supposed to teach kids coordination, logic skills.

My son already knows that I am not his real father. But I feel the day will come when he asks me about Marcus, and that is the day I want to be prepared for. I believe in honesty, and besides, my son should know who and what his father was.

He really should've known better, Marcus. He really should've thought about where he was, how far he'd come, where he was going. I guess he figured he could sneak back to Eighteenth Street. But like I said, when I found him he was in the alley by the super-market, deep in our part of the neighborhood. Maybe he knew I was coming. Maybe he tried to avoid me by going deeper into where he should not have been. I don't know what that man was thinking. Maybe he was just high.

He had broken back into the apartment. I'd heard the blinds chatter and bind. I'd stepped into the living room and seen him standing there at our front window, a silhouette before a flood of orange streetlight.

"Get the fuck out of here," I told him, and started to run toward him. But Marcus was fast. He spun and stepped right out through the open window. I ran back into the bedroom and grabbed my sweat-pants and shirt.

"What happened?" Blanca asked.

"I'm tired of this shit," I told her. I threw my shoes on. "This is the last fucking time." I reached into the dresser drawer.

"It doesn't matter, Jesse," Blanca said. "Just don't do…" I don't know how Blanca was going to finish her sentence. I was out the door with a gun in my hand.

The gun was Ricardo's. It was the same .38 we'd had that night we went looking for Marcus. I knew a time like this would come. The baseball bat hadn't worked and neither had the threats. "Don't take it out unless you're going to use it," Ricardo had said. "Because once you take it out, you have to use it." I remembered that later, after the shot, as I lay in bed, wondering if I'd killed the man, feeling guilty as I prayed that I had.

The only reason I went down the alley was because just as I came out of the apartment a squad car turned up Oakley. A few seconds earlier and they would've seen me, holding the gun. I imagine the nickel plating reflecting the squad-car headlights as I step out of my apartment. But I came out a few seconds after they passed my door, and so I turned down the alley.

I expected him to be right there, somewhere close, maybe hiding among the garbage cans just around the corner. I held the gun in front of me, then did a quick duck-and-juke move around the first bank of cans. Nothing. I started walking, sure that he was long gone. I put the gun in my pocket.

I walked to the end of the block, listening to pigeons cooing as they slept on window ledges. I turned onto Twenty-Third Place and suddenly there he was. He was walking slowly, strolling down the center of the alley right behind Leavitt Street. He had on a white T-shirt; I could see him clearly in the streetlight. He was wearing dark blue pants. He was long, thin. He moved like a cat, his steps more inline than side-by-side.

I didn't say anything. I pulled the gun from my pocket and stepped into the alley. Marcus turned. I saw his eyes widen, the quick registering of who I was, that I was holding a gun. He turned and began to run. The sound sailed up the walls around us. I heard the pop dissipate as it rang into the open air above the apartment buildings. Marcus's leg was up. It just didn't seem to come down. Instead his whole body came down. I wonder how many people die with that same look of surprise.

I ran. I was three blocks from home. Traffic could be heard over on Western Avenue. Everything seemed louder than it should've been. I suddenly felt like I had to get to work, like I should hurry up and get dressed and get on the L. In my head I could still hear the shot, the way it climbed up the walls and then vanished. I turned the corner and stepped inside the apartment. I kicked off my shoes and sat on the side of the bed. I'd been holding the gun the entire time.

"What happened?" Blanca asked me. She was sitting up.

"Nothing," I told her. I was out of breath.

"You didn't do anything, did you?"

"No," I said.

I got up and put the gun in the dresser drawer.

"I thought I heard a gunshot."

"Must've been the traffic," I said.

I lay down. I was shaking. She was staring down at me. I could feel it.

"Jesse, what did you do?" she asked me.

"Nothing," I told her. "It's cold out there. I don't even know where he went. That guy's a fucking chameleon."

I could feel my heart pounding in my chest. I could even hear it in my breathing.

"Jesse, you know, he's just going through hard times," she said. "Just let him be. He'll get over it. I know him. I know how he is."

I turned my face into my pillow and closed my eyes. My wife

finally lay down. I took a deep breath, then another.

I've never told anyone about what I did. And whatever neighborhood talk there was seems to have been confined to Marcus's part of Pilsen. This is how it is when people have enemies. The gun still sits underneath my underwear, in my dresser drawer. For a few days my underwear smelled like gunpowder.

That was four months ago. Since then my wife has brought up Marcus only once, and even then it was to comment on something little Marcus did, how he "looked" like his father when he got frustrated. At night, though, each time there is a knock or a scrape near any window, my wife stirs. I can feel her wake up. I can feel her stop breathing for just a moment, as if even her breath gets in the way of what she thinks she hears.

I know she will start to suspect something, eventually. I know she will begin to suspect. And when she asks, I will not tell her I killed the man she loves. But my son I feel I must tell, at some point. Just so that he knows his father loves him. Just so that he knows his father would do anything for his family.

SUPERNATURAL

Only a miracle could draw people to that canal. It has been forgotten about, shut off from the main river years ago, left as a depository of dumped appliances, cars, street-gang hits.

It's the perfect ghetto miracle. The toxic haze glowing bright green as if its light were filtered through emeralds. Maybe the years of dumped chemical solvents from the factory alongside it have finally yielded the kind of catastrophe scientific experts have anticipated for years. But this catastrophe is beautiful. A fluorescent haze that comes into sight each night, deepening as the heat of the day settles around the neighborhood.

They've been coming here for a week, the crowds, getting larger each successive night. The canal banks can barely hold the masses of people now. The spectators have begun spilling over into the factory's gravel parking lot, onto the bridge that spans the canal, onto Thirty-First Street, filling it in for blocks, as if in exodus.

Word has obviously gotten around. Probably passed along the front stoops of the neighborhood like hot merchandise. Down Twenty-Sixth Street, past the Cook County lockup, past the taco stands, the corner taverns, the story indulged a little more with every pass and reception: *The glow's deep, man, I mean deep. People are being cured and shit. Lil' Ralphy can walk again.*

The words would have sailed over the junkyards, the sleeping drunks, the trade school, the abandoned drive-in. They would've come to rest at Cicero Avenue, where the ghetto stops and a vast field of open prairie spans from there to the next neighborhood. The words would've mixed in with other marooned statements, the old news that had come to rest there, no one left to listen: *Crazy Frankie shot Player. Got me some wicked shit. The bitch is dead.*

Memo, everyone agrees, should've been the first to appear, charging money for canal-side seats, a dollar a pop, like he charges for his snow-cone *raspas*, his cucumber *pepinos*, every time there's a police investigation. With his nose for disaster, kids spend their summer days following him around the neighborhood, cheering when he starts his sprints, which sometimes last for blocks, ending at the next brutal event. His swift parades flash between buildings. His handcart bells jingle. His red baseball cap beckons the kids to follow. Eventually they stop at some place where there's blood in the street and Memo starts to call out, "*Raspas! Pepinos!*" not even winded. The kids, panting, lean up against each other and savor the carnage. Sometimes, if they have money, they pitch in and actually buy something.

But Memo, even with his nose attuned as it is to moneymaking opportunities, couldn't detect the event, didn't. And the brujas didn't either, the back-alley witches of K-Town, where all the witches are said to live, drawing power from the uniformity of the street names—Karlov, Kedvale, Keeler. And maybe, at the heart of it, this is the appeal of the green glow. How those normally attuned to the supernatural, those who seem to have a "sixth sense," seem dumbstruck, as if it were beyond their comprehension.

The event has taken on an air of revival. Estranged family members are reunited, quarreling relatives embrace, old partners, gangbangers, are brought back together as if their differences, their knife fights, their nights spent hunting for each other with baseball bats, had never occurred. "Just like old times," they say to each other. And this phrase permeates the crowd. Husbands are reunited with the mothers of their children. Boyfriends hug ex-common-law wives. The night becomes one big flashback. Everyone sliding one step back to a time when they were happy, or at least thought so.

Around nine o'clock, when the buzz of the insects turns to a strong throb, and the sun, somewhere behind all the haze, the buildings and church steeples, starts to set, the crowd quiets, and a flicker of green starts to snap at the center of the canal, just above the water. The flicker jerks and twists, then explodes into an opaque globe of light, strong, like a spirit, like you expect it to talk—but it doesn't. It just hovers there, casting a white light that passes into green as it reaches the crowd. The pulse of the insects fades, conversations, thoughts, movements stop, and a dullness takes over.

A freeze-frame, a wide-angled freeze-frame showing the long expanse of Thirty-First Street, its corridor of streetlights stretching into the horizon, would show the crowds en route. It would show them all staring up, pointing as if at fireworks, a glaze across their eyes as if they were under mass hypnosis. Some would be caught with their mouths open, black gapes, white teeth catching the light, streetlight maybe, but maybe the light of the glow as well.

Young women would be caught looking innocent. Those with tattooed tears, those holding babies, would be caught looking like their children, sharing their defenselessness, their vulnerability. And the young men too would be caught smiling the way gangsters do when some truth is revealed—innocently, giving one the slightest hope that they could be reasoned with, "saved," as some of their mothers might say. Of course, they never can be. Gangster faces change like masks. They're defense mechanisms. But in the freeze-frame the gangsters would be caught red-handed, smiling like bashful teenagers, as if they've suddenly found the right answer to a math problem on the blackboard before a class of schoolmates raised from the dead.

In the freeze-frame, Thirty-First Street would be crowded, ready to burst its sides and collapse the walls of the abandoned buildings that line its sidewalks. The exodus might be confused with any other pilgrimage, quests to view saints, kiss the feet of monks, to discover the meaning of life in deserts in Saudi Arabia, atop mountains in South America.

At the bottom of the freeze-frame, those closest to the glow have begun to take seats, resigned to the thought that they won't get any closer, overwhelmed by whatever the green glow holds.

And this goes on all night, through the heat. The drunks stay awake. The clergy from the local churches lead prayer sessions. Memo, the *vendedor*, stands there, his band of children crowded around him. The witches' assistants scan the crowd for more faces, those of the dead, the forgotten, more of whom seem to appear each night.

As morning comes, the very first tinges of light sliding up the horizon, the green glow begins to fade, and so does the mystery of whatever brought the people here. Shadows give way to starkness, reality, and slowly the people begin to move, some slower than others, embarrassed by their own gullibility. As they make their way back up Thirty-First Street to their sweatbox apartments, they crowd in closer, like cattle, seeking safety in numbers. They avoid eye contact, slouch as if hung over. They carry their sleeping children, the mothers following the fathers, everything in reverse. There is an aura of defeat to the crowd. Truth becomes apparent. There is only heat to look forward to, days spent at work, in factories, as secretaries, days spent in bed, days spent watching Memo charge up and down side streets, days spent believing in God, witches, prayer, the coming of another night.

ICE CASTLES

On the south side of Chicago, at Harlem Avenue and Archer, Joe and Frank's Meat Market pumps out smoked kielbasas like clockwork. Every Wednesday and Friday the smell of burning hickory fills the intersection. If the air is stagnant, smoke billows from Joe and Frank's chimney and fills the street corner like fog. But when the wind is up, the smoke carries. I live in Berwyn, a full three miles north of Joe and Frank's, and still, on a good day, with a gust of wind from the Bedford Park Intermodal, a blast of air from the Sanitary and Ship Canal, I can pick up the scent of Joe and Frank's. It reminds me of my childhood and of Pilsen.

Pilsen was marooned by relics, locked in by ancient industry. To the north was the old C, B & Q Railroad yard, rusted arrays of tracks twenty or thirty sets wide. To the east was the Chicago River and its permanently raised bridges. And to the south was Twenty-Second Street and its mile-long stretch of power plants, vacant warehouses, and junkyards. Pilsen was tall, dense, massive. The only reprieve was the uniformity: the open-air gangways that matched up perfectly from block to block, the side streets that ran uninterrupted through Pilsen. At any point in the neighborhood, down these corridors, our borders were in full view: the abandoned bridges at the river, the terrifyingly dark viaducts at Seventeenth Street, and above it all the fuming smokestacks of Twenty-Second Street.

Our houses were our reflections, cramped, utilitarian. We lived atop one another in wood-frame, two- and three-flat apartment buildings, clapboard siding like stereo-sundials as the sun rose and set. All of our houses were off-kilter somehow, a limping back porch, front steps crumbling and broken like ancient ruins. In some cases the flaws were inside, like in our apartment, where I could roll a penny in the kitchen and have it continue through the living room, pick up speed in the bedroom, and, if the back door was open, hop the threshold right out onto the porch. Pilsen had its share of stone-faced buildings, storefronts, brick churches, corner tenements, but these were torn up as well, mortar dark and broken like rotting teeth, soot rising in columns from wall-mounted chimneys. Pilsen was dark, forever. We lived in shadows with railroad tracks beneath our feet, tracks that ended at walled-off docks or rusted-over bumpers or sometimes at nothing at all, two lines side by side cut off in the middle of a street, traffic beating the ends into the asphalt, burying them slowly, inch by inch, like the whole city was sinking, Pilsen first.

Back then my father was a cab driver. He was in school studying to be a social worker. I didn't see him much. My mother was a secretary. She worked at an insurance agency, a social-service agency, the phone company: she changed jobs so often I stopped wondering where she worked. She would sigh as we ate dinner alone in our tiny kitchen. Sometimes I would sigh back. "Bad day?" my mother would ask.

"Yes," I would answer.

"Me too," she would say.

There was nothing excessive about my family's existence. We didn't go out for breakfast. We didn't order Chinese food. We ate beans and tortillas, fried potatoes, the occasional egg with my mother's green salsa. My mother made one thing each Sunday without fail, a pot of *frijoles*, and in the winter the kitchen window would fog over with steam and the house would smell of garlic and onions. In the summer when all the windows of the neighborhood were open and all of Pilsen was making its *frijoles* for the week, the whole neighborhood smelled of garlic and onions.

Memories of my father during this time are sparse. I used to see him asleep on the couch as I got ready for school. Sometimes I would wake to use the bathroom and he would be at the kitchen table eating leftovers. The streetlight outside would illuminate our white curtain; our white table would reflect the dim light of the kitchen. My father would watch me walk across the kitchen and into the bathroom. Then, when I was done, he'd watch me walk back across the kitchen, everything in total silence, like he was afraid to speak. As it stands, most of our encounters during this period seem more like dreams than actual memories. And really what seems most stark about those memories is the checkered-flag floor in our old kitchen, the tall, rotted step to get up into the bathroom, the painted-over hook on the door, the orange streetlight shining through my mother's sheer curtain. The image of my father sitting there is so vague I've nearly forgotten it: my father is a forgotten dream, how much more detached can I be? But we had the fires, him and me. If not for the fires I might have forgotten who my father was altogether.

I am sure he spotted them while out on his route or maybe on his way home from the garage. What alerted me were his whispers: "Hey, want to go check out a fire?" With that I would sit up, throw on whatever clothes I could find, and off we'd go, down our apartment building's steps, out the front door, out into Pilsen. That first breath, that first inhale of charred wood, brought me back into the world. It was like morning coffee or that TV ad for hand soap where *"the scent opens your eyes."* With that first breath of burning wood, I could tell where I was again: *Pilsen, early morning, with my father. A house was burning.*

A big fire added halos around the streetlamps, smoke hanging in the air like the three-flats were skyscrapers. An even bigger fire brought flurries of ash like black snowflakes falling to the sherbet-tinted sidewalk. If the fire was close enough, it looked like a premature sunrise as we walked down May Street. Emergency lights, red, blue, white, filtered down the long, deep gangways like panels on a revolving lamp. We'd turn a corner or two and then we were there, flames roaring from windows, from roofs. Ladders, streams of water, wet pavement like sheets of polished glass cut by the thick, dark, inflated fire hoses.

There were no small fires in Pilsen. Our houses were like matchsticks, flammable and close together. Asphalt roofs, asphalt siding on wood frames, wood-framed porches, wood-beam floors: inevitably, during a fire, flames would jump to one or two neighboring buildings and then, as smoothly as a train leaves a station, the firefighters would pull their hoses across the mouth of the gangway, toss up new ladders, crash in windows, and begin the battle all over again.

Warehouse fires were the largest: three or four engines, water cannons, platforms, snorkels. The approach was different as well, constant streams of water, calm delivery. Floors collapsed, roofs collapsed, walls collapsed, but the firefighters took it all in stride, let it happen, talked, drank coffee, let the blaze wear itself out. In a house fire, a tenement fire, chaos was always about to break free. Windows were punched out, roofs were ripped open, walls were pulled down, all while melting asphalt dripped globs of flame from two- or three-story eaves. In a house fire, ladders got put up against windows and firefighters came down with squirming pets, crying survivors. Sometimes they came down with bodies, limp and unconscious. Sometimes the bodies were quite small. My father and I watched all this from a distance, in the galley of other witnesses, neighbors, aunts, uncles, unprepared fathers, sons, fire chasers, folks on the way home from third-shift jobs they took just to get by, to survive, paying rent on a lopsided, creaking-in-the-wind, tinderbox apartment. We stood shoulder to shoulder, saw each other sometimes twice a week, in the winter when the kerosene heaters started up and the fires got more frequent, but we never spoke, barely exchanged a glance. The galley was anonymous. We were all from Pilsen, that much I knew.

Waking up after a fire was always rough. It was like I needed a breath of charred wood, a first inhale, to ease me back into life. Instead it was the doldrums of a regular day, my father on the couch, puffed-rice cereal, my mother driving me to school. Sometimes we would pass the night's burned-out remains and for a moment I'd have a flash, a spark of memory that brought me back to reality, though which reality I wasn't quite sure. *I was standing here a few hours ago. I saw this building in flames.* The blackened space was sometimes a confirmation, more so if the actual structure was still intact, but the memory never seemed any more real than a dream, any more real than my memories of my father. As we drove past I would intentionally turn away. Back then it seems I lived life night to night rather than day to day.

The blaze I remember most happened during the winter. The building was a four-flat with a stone facade. It had a straight roofline with brackets holding up the ledge, like on an Old West saloon. As far as Pilsen goes, it was one of the more modern buildings. Across the street was Gracie's, the laundromat my mother used when Mable's on Eighteenth was crowded. While waiting for clothes, I'd look directly out onto the building, watch families pass, walk into Zemsky's next door, then walk out and pass the building again. The building was taller than either of its neighbors. It looked squeezed in, muscled in, like it was taller only because of the pressure to either side. When you took in the panoramic view, the building's situation seemed even more unfair. Blue Island Avenue was an angled street. The blocks were extra long, extra crowded. This was the only stretch of Pilsen with no gangways to separate buildings, no breathing room. The building was crammed, suffocated. Pilsen was crowded enough without angled streets thrown into the mix.

I can't remember seeing anyone specific living there. I am sure there were children in there, old folks, laborers. It was a Pilsen flat. There were probably eight apartments, ten including the basement boiler room and attic space, which the landlord would have rented out for less than full rent. There was one front door. One center staircase, I'm sure, accessed by long hallways. It was a real tenement. The kind that had a common bathroom at one point. The kind of invisible building that you stepped into and disappeared. The kind of time-warp building that made people say "Damn, where have you been?" when they saw you back on the street.

I knew it was big. When my father and I stepped out of our building I could smell the cinder, strong and hard rather than soft and sweet. Black snowflakes were falling and the cold was sharp enough that I was relieved to climb into the car, which was still warm from my father's drive home. My father said there was lots of equipment there already, and when we pulled up there were at least three ladder trucks, plus three pumper trucks. But the building was a lost cause. Flames were shooting through the windows. The roof had disintegrated, flames were flapping above the roofline. The white facade of the building stood out gray and dingy in the spotlights from the squad cars, the fire engines. Against the cold the fire seemed to bite even more. Each lick of fire seemed like a slice against the winter sky. And the water didn't seem to help. Firefighters shot water through the windows. Up high there was a cannon shooting water down through what used to be the roof. But the fire kept on burning, blazing, like it *wanted* to burn. Or maybe it was Pilsen. Maybe Pilsen needed the burn, just for the heat.

The usual collection of victims with blankets, in nightgowns, pajamas, wasn't there. Instead it was just us, the residents of Pilsen, the galley, some of us sitting in cars, some of us standing, steam highlighting our exhalations. Whoever was in the building was still in there, had to be, and as the minutes wore on a column of flame took hold. By the time we left, the building looked like a four-story jack-o'-lantern.

We went home, and while my father warmed up his dinner I climbed into bed. I knew he would not want to disturb my mother. That he would sleep on the couch and that my mother would wake up and our awkwardness as a family would continue for one more day. I could smell the fire, the charred wood, in my nose, on my arms, like I was burning, like I had been in the blaze myself. A building that tall and narrow was complicated to navigate even without fire. It was a wormhole, a building you stepped into and never came out of.

The next morning I awoke and found my father still asleep on the couch. I went to the table, got my bowl of puffed rice. I could still smell the blaze. My jacket was hanging on the chair but the smell was something stronger, like my father was also coated with it, the whole house, like the smell had finally become a part of all three of us.

"Did you guys go out last night?" my mother asked me.

"Yes," I said.

"Which building was it?"

"The one across from the laundromat," I said. "The tall one by Zemsky's."

"I never saw anyone go in there," my mother answered.

"Me neither," I said.

My mother and I exited our building out into the cold morning. We climbed into the car, the same one I had been in just a few hours before, though now it was cold, needing time to warm up. We drove down Eighteenth Street, turned onto Blue Island. There was the building, the shell of the building, coated in ice, transformed, glimmering, beautiful in the morning sun, an ice castle waiting to be occupied by anyone desperate enough to live there.

ABOUT THE AUTHOR

Alexai Galaviz-Budziszewski grew up in the Pilsen neighborhood on the south side of Chicago. He has taught in the Chicago public school system and is currently a high school counselor for students with disabilities. In his spare time he builds and repairs motorcycles.